MERCENARY IN LOVE 2

J.L. ROSE
J.L. TURNER

GOOD 2 GO PUBLISHING

Mercenary In Love 2
Written by J.L. Rose & J.L. Turner
Cover Design: Davida Baldwin – Odd Ball Designs
Typesetter: Mychea
ISBN: 978-1-947340-41-1
Copyright © 2019 Good2Go Publishing
Published 2019 by Good2Go Publishing
7311 W. Glass Lane • Laveen, AZ 85339
www.good2gopublishing.com
https://twitter.com/good2gobooks
G2G@good2gopublishing.com
www.facebook.com/good2gopublishing
www.instagram.com/good2gopublishing

Dedications

This book is dedicated to God, my family, and to my heart and soon-to-be wife, Jazz. I love you and will always be there for you as long as God gives me life. I promise my life on that!

J.L. Rose

This book is first dedicated to my Heavenly Father, but also to both my mother and sister. I love you both and thank you for always being there for me. Also, to J.L. Rose, you really came through with this one as you said you would, and I thank you greatly. Last and most important, to my lover and best friend: Baby, I will always and forever love you. Thank you for loving me and allowing me to love you. Thank you!

J.L. Turner

MERCENARY IN LOVE 2

ONE

After the scene at Menace's girlfriend's house, Mia was completely pissed off after Sean's last words to her, and the fact that he actually felt that she cared more for her job than for her life with him. Mia made it into her apartment and stormed into the bedroom, where she threw down her things before she fell across her bed and growled almost in a scream.

She heard her phone ring moments after lying down. She rolled over and got back up to answer her phone, and saw that Jennifer was calling.

"Yeah, Jennifer?"

"Wow! Why do you sound like that? What happened now?"

"Girl, I don't know what to do with Sean!" Mia told her

friend and partner.

She then went into detail about their meeting with the guy named Menace and the way Sean acted to get information out of him. She even told Jennifer about Sean's last words to her and her question she asked him to which he didn't respond.

"So you think Sean believes you love your job more than you love him?" Jennifer asked once Mia was finished.

"You really need to ask that question, Jennifer?" Mia asked. "It's obvious what Sean is thinking, and I don't like it!"

"Maybe you're thinking about this all wrong, Mia! Maybe Sean just wants to make sure you have a job when this is all over, or maybe he doesn't want to be a problem for you."

2

After listening to Jennifer and considering the possibility that she was right, Mia didn't want to discuss the issue anymore and changed the subject.

"Have you decided what you're taking on this trip?"

"Have you even talked to Sean or Luther yet about all of this, Mia?"

"Shit!" Mia cried at the mention of Luther's name. She checked her phone and saw that, in fact, he had called her twice. "Jennifer, let me call you back!"

~ ~ ~

Sean switched from Nina's loud-colored car to T.J.'s dark blue '87 Crown Vic that looked black in the dark. Sean found the address that Menace had given him to locate Marcus. He then drove past the pool hall and realized it was the spot at which Marcus was known to hang out.

Sean found a place to park the Crown Vic right behind the hall and in front of a pink-and-white house. He climbed out of the car and slipped back on his jacket, and then slid Menace's .45 into his jeans at his back before locking up the Crown Vic.

He walked back around to the front of the pool hall and followed a brown-skinned woman and her friend inside. He paused inside the door to allow his eyes to adapt to the dimly lit room. Once his eyes had adjusted, Sean walked around the tables searching for the familiar face of Marcus.

He spotted Marcus after a few minutes at the back of the room, which was actually one of the darkest areas inside. Sean ran a quick count of nine guys and four women that were with Marcus playing pool, drinking, and smoking.

Sean cared nothing about the friends. He walked over

to the pool table, and in the middle of Marcus making a shot, he snatched up a pool stick from the next table and tossed it onto the table, which messed up Marcus's shot.

"What the fuck!" Marcus yelled as he shot upright, looking around and yelling. "Who the fuck threw this fucking stick?"

"What's up, Marcus?" Sean asked as he walked into the light provided by the pool table's overhead light. "Remember me?"

"Who the fuck is you?" Marcus asked, squinting his eyes to see who the new voice belonged to.

He leaned forward into the light when the familiar face appeared in his view.

"Get the fuck outta here! This muthafucker gotta be fucking crazy or just stupid as fuck walking up in this bitch by his muthafucking self!"

"Marcus, ain't this that same fuckin' nigga from the club the other night?" Marcus heard his boy, Pistol Paul ask. He laughed as he stepped around the table and approached Sean. "So, how's that soft-ass nigga Tony and his bitch-ass homeboy T.J. doing?" he cockily asked.

Moving before T.J.'s name completely left Marcus's mouth, Sean punched him in the throat and then quickly grabbed him by the back of the head while Marcus was choking. He slammed Marcus's head facedown onto the edge of the pool table.

Sean ducked the swing he caught out of the corner of his eye from Pistol Paul. Sean then smashed a solid right to homeboy's mid-section, only to stand up and hook his right arm around the guy's throat while facing him. He swung and sent Paul in a half backflip backward onto the pool table behind him.

Sean put in the work defending himself, even though it seemed as though he was always on the offensive end of the fight. He broke one guy's arm at the elbow by breaking it inward from the back end, and even pulled down an overhead light above another pool table after kicking another guy onto the table. Sean stood looking around at each of Marcus's friends that were laid out across the pool hall floor. He shook his head as he turned his attention back onto Marcus, who was still unconscious.

Sean walked over and picked up Marcus and slapped him awake, ignoring the painful moaning.

"Wake up!"

Sean slapped Marcus even harder and woke the boy up

completely.

Sean then shook his head and said, "I got a little something better for you! Let's go see an old friend."

~ ~ ~

Sean exited the pool hall with Marcus and drove back across town after calling up his cousin to have him meet up at the spot in Overtown. Sean pulled up in front of the apartment and saw Tony and the rest of the team already out front waiting on him.

"What's up, Cuz?" Tony called out after Sean parked and climbed out from the Crown Vic. "What's so important you got us all out here his late?"

"Just a little surprise!" Sean answered as he walked around to the passenger side of the car and pulled Marcus out.

"What the fuck?" T.J. yelled out, laughing after seeing

who Sean had snatched from the Crown Vic. "This nigga

Sean is crazy as fuck! Fam went and snatched this nigga

Marcus's ass up!"

"Where you find this muthafucker?" Tony asked as

Sean walked up and tossed a beat-the-fuck-up Marcus to the

ground at his feet.

"Pool hall!" Sean answered. "I decided to let you and

T.J. deal with this one since his ass wanted to play the

background and send a hit man to do his job."

"What about that clown Menace?" T.J. wanted to know.

"I got that one!" Sean replied, looking back as three

different rides pulled up from around the corner.

"That's them niggas. It's A.J. and them from the county

that got out with us!" T.J. explained as the rest of his boys climbed from their rides.

Sean shook up with the guys he had met and remembered from the county jail. He then stood kicking it a few minutes with the crew, but before he broke off to head for home, he pulled his cousin to the side.

"What's good, cuz?" Tony asked, once he and Sean stood a few feet away from each other.

"Listen!" Sean started.

He then explained to Tony that he was going to work something out with a friend to see if he could get his cousin a stronger connect and backup that would keep him and the rest of the team out of jail and off the police radar while they were out in the streets getting hustlers money.

After sharing a few more words with Tony and then hugging his cousin before taking off, Sean yelled to T.J. that he would bring him back the car later in the afternoon. He turned to walk back out to the Crown Vic and caught the eyes of Nina, who was staring hard and angrily at him.

Sean shook his head, climbed into the car, and decided to deal with Nina at a later date.

~ ~ ~

Mia was unable to sleep and began to worry even more than she already was. She threw the blanket off of her and got out of bed to head to the bathroom, just as she heard her cell phone begin to ring.

She rushed back over to the bed and dove across it to snatch up her cell phone.

"Hello?" Mia answered breathing heavily.

"Come open the door."

"Sean?" she cried out, only to hear the line die.

Mia tossed down the phone and rushed from the bedroom, out to the front room, and up to the front door. She unlocked the door and snatched it open, just as Sean stopped right in front of it.

"Oh my God!" she cried as she threw her arms up around his neck.

Mia allowed Sean to pick her up as she wrapped her legs around his waist, lay her head on his shoulder, and rested her face in the crack of his neck.

"You miss me, huh?" Sean asked her after locking the front door.

The two of them then started down the hall to the back of the apartment.

"Sean, I was worried!" Mia explained, lifting her head to meet his eyes. "Baby, don't ever not answer your phone when I call you. Please, Sean!"

Sean kissed Mia's forehead and then made the promise to do as she asked of him.

TWO

Sean heard his phone ring, which woke him up from his sleep. He opened his eyes to find himself staring directly at his cell phone that was on the night table. He started to reach for it, just as another arm reached across him and snatched up the phone.

"Hello?" Sean heard, confused a few brief moments until he turned over to see Mia beside him talking on his cell phone.

Everything came back to him as he remembered he was at Mia's apartment. He sat up and listened to her as she spoke on the phone with who he now knew was Luther Simmons.

"Hey, you!" Mia said, smiling up at Sean after hanging up with Luther.

She sat up and wrapped her arms around his neck and pulled him down to kiss her.

After sitting back up after the kiss had ended, Sean asked, "So, what did Luther want?"

"Oh, he just asked if I wanted to go to Costa Rica."

"And you agreed?"

"Wasn't that the plan?"

"I wasn't sure we had plans, Mia."

Hearing Sean's tone and sitting up to get a better look at him, Mia smiled and realized something.

"Baby, you're jealous!"

"Jealous of what?" Sean stated as he got out of bed

and headed to the bathroom.

Mia smiled as she sat up watching her extremely handsome boyfriend as he walked into the bathroom. She got up and followed behind him. She found him standing in front of the toilet using it.

"So, you're jealous, Sean?"

"Where are you getting this from?" he asked, looking back over his shoulder at Mia. "What reason would I have for being jealous, Mia?"

"Okay!" she replied, still smiling as she stood watching him walk over to the sink to wash his hands. "So, has Luther asked you yet about your date?"

"I haven't spoken to him since our last visit together," Sean answered as he headed out of the bathroom. "I gotta call him up today, matter of fact."

"Well, I spoke to Jennifer, and she agreed to be your date for the trip," Mia told him, catching the look Sean shot her as she passed him at the bed, hiding the smile from him upon seeing that he was clearly jealous.

~ ~ ~

Sean took off to his own place to shower and change clothes. He switched from the outfit he had worn the night before into some dark gray sweatpants, a gray wifebeater, and a pair of white ankle socks. He then grabbed his cell phone and fell into his sofa to make his call to Luther.

He listened to the line ring as he switched on the news in his den on his flat-screen wall unit. He smiled after seeing the news report about a body being found and identified as Marcus Cook.

"Simmons here!" Sean heard through the line. It was Luther.

"What's up, Luther? I see you called last night."

"Sean Carter!" Luther stated, sounding as if he was smiling. "I was wondering what happened to you. Everything all right?"

"It is now!"

"That's good to hear," Luther replied before he asked, "So, have you found someone for our trip out to Costa Rica? I've already told Tiffany, and she's all excited and ready to go."

"I've got someone!" Sean admitted. "I just need to

call and get her answer after you and I finish talking."

"Well, what time can you get to my house? We've

got a few things to handle today?"

"I need to find a new car first, but then I'll be right

over."

"What happened to your Porsche?"

"It was totaled last night while I was dealing with a

family issue."

"I see!" Luther replied. "I tell you want, Sean. Go

and see the guy I took you to when we got you the

Porsche. He'll be waiting on you and pick out whatever

you want, but remember you represent me now, Sean.

Keep that in mind!"

After hanging up with Luther Simmons after a few

more minutes, Sean called up Michael Brown to ask a favor before contacting Jennifer about joining him on the trip to Costa Rica.

~ ~ ~

After hanging up the phone with her boss, after further informing him on the details of the trip including the locations where the trip was taking place, Mia tried calling Jennifer and ended up getting her voice message. She left her den and went to fix something to eat, deciding on a cold cut sandwich and a bag of chips that she had inside her cabinet.

Mia then grabbed a glass of orange juice and walked back into her den. She tried calling Jennifer again and ended up getting her voice message a second time.

"What in the world?" she said, tossing her phone down onto the sofa, only for the thing to begin ringing.

Mia picked up the phone again and saw that it was Jennifer calling back.

"I just called you a few minutes ago," Mia answered.

"Mia, hold on!"

Pausing in the middle of taking a bite of her sandwich, after hearing and recognizing the man's voice who answered her friend's phone, Mia called out to Sean. She had heard him in the background talking to Jennifer, who began to giggle.

"Hello!" Jennifer said into the phone, still giggling

and laughing. "Mia, you there?"

"What is Sean doing answering your phone, Jennifer? Where the hell are you?"

"Mia, relax, girl! We're just at the mall shopping."

"At the mall?"

"Yeah! Sean took me shopping for our trip to Costa Rica. He wanted me to have some stuff when we left, so he took me to the mall to shop."

"I can't believe this shit!" Mia announced, looking at the phone and really not liking the way she was feeling at the moment. She got back onto the phone and said, "Jennifer, look! Just call me when you're done shopping with Sean."

After hanging up the phone and giving Jennifer no

chance to say anything else, Mia tossed down her cell phone. She was no longer hungry after just finding out that her boyfriend was out treating her friend to a shopping spree.

~ ~ ~

Sean got Jennifer back to her place after taking her shopping. He then met up with Michael Brown at their normal dinner spot. He called Tony beforehand to let his cousin know when and where to meet him.

"Business must be going well," Michael Brown said. He then nodded toward a new black-on-black matted Bentley Continental GT that was parked out in front of the diner. "Nice new wheels you got there. What happened to the Porsche?"

"Got tired of it!" Sean replied before he changed the subject. "So, you thought about my favor?"

"I'm here, aren't I?" Michael replied. "I'm only doing this because you're Jeffery's boy and you're asking, but business is business no matter who this guy is to you. We clear?"

Sean slowly nodded his head as he looked out the window and saw Hulk's truck pull up. Sean announced his cousin's arrival and watched as Tony and Hulk climbed from the SUV and started toward the entrance of the diner.

Sean held up his hand to get his cousin's attention when Tony walked in. Sean waved him over to the table where he and Michael were waiting.

"What's up, Cuz?" Tony began, greeting Sean with an embrace.

Sean then introduced Tony and Michael to one another.

"I've got other business to handle, but I'll get back with you two later."

Once he got outside, Sean walked over toward Hulk and whispered, "I expect you to watch my cousin's back. Do we agree on that?"

"Till death do our asses part, fam!" Hulk replied as he and Sean shook up.

Sean nodded to Tony and Michael from outside as he was leaving. He then dug out his cell phone and pulled up Luther's number as he was climbing into his new car.

"Simmons."

"I'm on my way now."

"Change of plans, Sean. I'm glad you called. I'm on

my way to see about a really good friend of mine. I just

got a call that he was having a problem with some

gangs around the area. Meet me in ten minutes at

Dino's"

"Where at?" Sean asked, listening to Luther give

the address to where he was supposed to meet him.

~ ~ ~

Luther arrived at the restaurant owned and run by

his two friends. He waited until Frank opened the car

door for him, and he stepped out of his Rolls-Royce to

a waiting team of eight men on his security team.

"Hey, Mr. Simmons," a few people called out his name, to whom he nodded and waved at a few faces he remembered but did not know.

He then noticed that one of the front windows was being replaced as he entered the restaurant that was full as always.

"Luther!"

Luther smiled at the sight of Simone, Dino's wife of more than twenty-three years. Luther then hugged the still gorgeous Italian and white-mixed woman.

"Simone, you still look beautiful!" he told her, stepping back to look over the forty-three-year-old beauty.

"I've still got my eye on you, Simmons," Luther

heard, recognizing the voice behind him and smiling as

he turned around to see his friend and business

partner.

"Dino, how's it going, my friend?" Luther asked as

he and Dino embraced each other. "Business looks

good!"

"Business is okay," Dino replied with an

expression that showed his displeasure. "Look at the

window, Luther. These thugs have got to be stopped

or business will be no more!"

"Luther!" Simone spoke up, drawing his attention.

"We received a message just yesterday demanding that

we pay $50,000 each month or our business will be

shut down. We really need your help!"

Luther felt a tap on his shoulder just as he was about to respond. He looked back at Frank to see his head of security nod toward the door. Looking to where Frank was nodding, Luther slowly smiled when he saw Sean step into the restaurant dressed in a dark blue tailored designer suit and square-toed leather shoes that looked really good on the young man.

Luther waved and got Sean's attention. He looked back at Simone and Dino and said, "I want you two to relax. I've got someone to fix this problem quickly and very quietly."

Once Sean walked up beside him, Luther introduced both Dino and Simone to Sean, and then he spoke up, "Both Dino and Simone are very close friends of mine, Sean. They're having a problem with this group that calls themselves the Beachside Gangsters. I need you to deal with them in a permanent way. Do you get my drift?"

"Where can I find these guys?" Sean asked, looking directly at Dino.

~ ~ ~

After leaving Luther at the restaurant with his friends, Sean drove out to the park where he was informed the Beachside Gangsters hung out. He also noticed the huge crowd as he pulled up in front of the park.

He drove around to the parking lot and noticed

that he was drawing attention from members of the crowd. Sean parked the Bentley, climbed out, and fixed his suit jacket before closing the car door.

Sean left the Bentley and walked over to the crowd that was gathered around the bleacher area, paying no attention to the way everyone was now staring at him. He just walked right up into the group.

"Dude, you gotta be lost!" one of the male members stated while looking Sean over in the suit he was wearing. "Ain't no church out this way. But we got a whole lot of trouble if that's what you're looking to get into."

"I'm looking for the one that calls himself Rasco," Sean said, noticing the way the crowd reacted to the name.

"Why you looking for Rasco, my boy?" another member spoke up.

Sean shifted his attention to the guy that asked the question and was seated between two females.

"You Rasco?" Sean asked.

"Who wants to know?" the guy asked, nodding his head and causing four of his boys to shift and cycle around homeboy in the designer suit.

Sean ignored the circle of men that he was now placed in the middle of, and answered the question he was asked.

"I'm here to speak with you about the Gambainos who own the Italian restaurant a few blocks from where we are now."

"You better leave our money, or we're sending your ass back with holes in ya!" another member threatened.

He then pulled out a switchblade and waved it, getting a few laughs from his crew.

Sean shifted his eyes to the guy on his left with the knife. He swiftly stepped into a spinning back kick that caught the guy to the chest. The homeboy stumbled back, only to fall straight to his knees holding his chest in pain and unable to breathe.

He caught the whole crew off guard, and now he stood up in the same spot holding his Ruger 9 mm that he had gripped in his right hand down at his side against his thigh. Sean spoke up again instantly getting everyone's attention.

"Which one of you is Rasco?"

"So, who you supposed to be?" said the homeboy that sat between the two females, making the mistake of standing up as he continued. "I could give a fuck about all that Bruce Lee bullshit you came out here with. You just tell them Italian muthafuckers that by the end of this month, they better have my money or I'ma have something special for their ass!"

Sean had heard enough, and he was completely sure of who was standing up in front of him. He swung up the Ruger and pulled the trigger.

Boom!

Sean sent a bullet straight to Rasco's forehead, watching his body fall straight backward over the bleachers as the others took off running and screaming. Sean started back toward his car while digging out his phone to call and let Luther know the job was handled.

THREE

After the issue was handled for the Gambainos and the goodbyes were made, Luther waved Frank off when his head of security started to open the back door to the Rolls-Royce. Instead, Luther informed Frank that he would be riding with Sean.

As Luther walked over to his new Bentley, he nodded his head in approval of the choice of cars that Sean had selected for himself. Luther then climbed inside and onto the peanut-butter-tan leather seats.

"Nice! Really nice!"

Sean glanced over at Luther as he started up the Bentley, and saw the guy looking around the car's interior.

Sean started to pull off just as Luther asked, "So, what exactly did you do to handle the issue with these Beachside Gangsters, Sean?"

Sean remained quiet for a few moments before he spoke.

"There's this old saying I heard some years ago. You kill the head and—!"

"The body's dead!" Luther finished for him, smiling at clearly understanding exactly what Sean meant.

"So tell me something, Luther," Sean began, getting Luther's attention. "I understand those two back there were your friends as you called them, but what's the real reason you went out of your way to handle a small issue like that, when you could have just sent a team over to deal with that crew and it would have been easier?"

"Well, truthfully, Sean, Dino and Simone are really good friends of mine, as I told you." Luther had made that perfectly clear, but he continued. "But you see, things are always business in this life of mine, Sean. Dino and Simone are one of the first businesses that I not only helped, but also that help me clean my dirty money. So now you understand why I had you handle an issue that I would rather keep quiet rather than having it blown out of the water."

Sean nodded his head in understanding. He also

understood that a large amount of Luther's money was not easily touched, since it was being washed through legitimate businesses. Sean now realized that what he needed to do was find out which businesses were working for Luther Simmons.

~ ~ ~

After dropping off Luther and agreeing to come back over with his date to eat dinner later that evening, Sean called up Jennifer to inform her of the plans for tonight.

"Hello!"

"Jennifer, this is Sean. You busy?"

"Hi, Sean. No, I'm not busy, but what's up?"

"Listen, do you got plans for tonight, cutie?"

"Why you asking?"

Sean explained everything about Luther's offer to have dinner at his place.

"It's a good chance for you and Mia to have a look around his place and do that special agent stuff y'all do."

"Bye, boy. I'll see you tonight when you call me."

~ ~ ~

"What the hell was that?" Mia went off after watching Jennifer the whole time she was on the phone with Sean, giggling and laughing. "What other Sean do you know, Jennifer?"

"Mia, please!" Jennifer said, waving her hand at her. "I only know one Sean, and that was him. I was only laughing because his butt is a trip, Mia! Sean keeps me laughing. But he called to ask me if I wanted to go to dinner with him tonight at Luther's house."

"Luther's house?" Mia repeated. "Why hasn't Luther called and asked me about going with him to have dinner?"

"Mia, I do not—!" Jennifer started, just as Mia's phone began to ring from on top of the coffee table in front of them.

She watched Mia pick up the phone and saw that it was, in fact, Luther Simmons calling her. Jennifer sat and listened to the one-sided phone conversation until Mia hung up a few minutes later.

"So what did he say?" she asked Mia.

"Luther just invited me over to his house for dinner tonight. He's sending a car over to pick me up from the apartment building where he thinks I live," Mia explained in a lowered voice, which caused Jennifer to burst out laughing.

"Girl, you are a trip!" Jennifer responded while still laughing at her.

~ ~ ~

Sean drove over and picked up his sister. He had planned to spend a little time with her and visit Ma'Pearl's house and hang out over there. Sean found himself being questioned about how things were going between him and Mia. He fed into the madness, giving his grandmother food to go back and feed to Mia's grandmother.

About twenty minutes after 6:00 p.m., Sean explained to his sister and grandmother that he had a date with Mia, and expressed that he needed to get home and start getting ready. Ma'Pearl told him that he could leave Tasha at her place and she would take her home, so he could leave to go get ready.

Sean kissed Ma'Pearl and Tasha goodbye and then left the house and started for home, making one stop at a flower shop he spotted and was surprised was still open.

Once he left the florist and finally made it back to his place, Sean made a quick stop at Mia's door without bothering to knock. He left a red rose and a card that read "I love you" on the door. He rode the elevator up to his own floor and began to get ready, dressing for his dinner date at Luther Simmons's mansion.

~ ~ ~

Mia looked herself over one last time in the mirror when the call from downstairs came to let her know that her ride was out front waiting for her. Mia picked up her purse and keys and then headed for the front door.

She turned out all the lights but the one in the kitchen and stepped out into the hallway. She was closing the door behind her when she spotted the red rose on top of a white card on the floor in front of her door.

She picked up the rose and card from the floor and opened it to see the simple message: I love you. Mia smiled when she saw Sean's name signed at the bottom of the card.

Mia put the card and rose inside her apartment and finally made it down to the lobby where her taxicab was waiting. Mia took the taxi over to the fake apartment where Luther thought she lived. Once she got out, she sighed that the car Luther was sending over for her was not there yet.

"Thanks!"

Mia made it to the front porch when she heard the car pull up behind her. Mia turned around and looked back out to the street to see Luther's Rolls-Royce and

Frank climbing from the passenger side of the car.

~ ~ ~

"Here I come!" Jennifer yelled from the front room inside her apartment, shutting off the lights after hearing the doorbell ring.

Jennifer grabbed her purse, cell phone, and keys and then rushed to the front door. There, she paused at the door to catch her breath a moment before she opened the door.

"Hi!" She greeted Sean with a big smile as she took him in, dressed amazingly in a cream-colored Tom Ford suit and suede shoes. "You look really handsome, Sean."

"I was just thinking the same thing about you,"

Sean admitted. "I was just thinking more so on the lines of beautiful or, better yet, gorgeous."

"Boy, come on!" Jennifer said, blushing as she stepped outside while shutting the front door behind her.

While being escorted out to Sean's new Bentley, Jennifer thanked him for opening her door for her, but then broke out in a huge smile when he leaned into the car and came back out with a pink rose that he handed to her.

"Thank you, Sean!" Jennifer said, blushing even harder after accepting the beautiful rose from him.

Once they were inside the car and Sean was pulling away from in front of her building, Jennifer started to ask him a personal question, only for Sean to speak up first and say, "I figured out how Luther is cleaning his money."

"We already knew how, Sean!" Jennifer informed him. "We just haven't figured out what businesses he's using to clean his dirty money."

"I may be able to help you out a little there!" Sean told Jennifer as he then went into detail about the Gambaino's restaurant, to which he gave her the address and names of the owners.

"How'd you find this out?" she asked after writing down the information Sean had just given her.

"Let's just say he and I had a little talk after leaving the restaurant," Sean told her, cutting his eyes over to

Jennifer while winking at her.

~ ~ ~

Sean reached Luther's mansion and saw a few other cars already there. He pulled up to the front door, only to have one of Luther's servants walk out and open up Jennifer's door for her. Sean then climbed out from behind the wheel, just as another car pulled up.

"Mr. Simmons is awaiting all guests inside the sitting room," the servant told Sean, remembering him from other visits.

After thanking the man and taking Jennifer's hand, Sean escorted her into the mansion and saw other guests walking around.

"Wow!" Jennifer said in shock after entering the

front door. "At least Simmons has good taste!"

"He does!" Sean admitted while staring hard and straight at Luther and Mia, with Luther's arm around her waist while his hand rested on the top curve of her right butt cheek.

"Calm down, Sean!" Jennifer told him after spotting Mia and noticing the way Sean was staring at her. "Mia's working, Sean! Please do not overreact tonight."

"I'm good!" Sean responded as he led Jennifer into the sitting room with the other guests.

~ ~ ~

Mia spotted Sean and Jennifer as soon as the two of them entered the room. Mia stood staring at how good they looked together, wearing almost the same

exact color and holding hands. She tried to control

herself and what she was feeling, just as Luther noticed

Sean calling him over.

"I see you finally made it," Luther said as Sean

walked over with his date. He shook hands with Sean,

but then looked over at his date and said, "Impressive,

Sean. You've got amazing taste, my friend."

"Thanks!" Sean replied, but then added, "I see you

had to outdo us all with the most gorgeous woman in

the room tonight, huh?"

He looked at Tiffany and saw her blushing.

Luther smiled, only to quickly change the subject

and say, "Well, as you can see, we have some very

important people in the house tonight, Sean. Come and

I'll introduce you to a few."

After introducing each other's dates to one

another, Sean and Luther excused themselves and

walked off. Mia and Jennifer then walked together and

spoke to each other in a lowered whisper.

"You recognize a few of these faces in here, don't

you, Jennifer?" Mia asked.

"A few isn't the word," Jennifer said, staring across

the room at the infamous Dante Blackwell and his just-

as-infamous wife, Alinna.

"I'm glad those two retired," Mia stated, seeing

who Jennifer was staring at.

"I was thinking the same thing. But why are they

here if they no longer live in Miami?" Jennifer

wondered out loud. "I thought they moved out to

Arizona to live."

"I heard it was New York," Mia said. "With those

two, nobody was ever able to keep up with their

movements."

Leaving the Blackwells alone, Mia and Jennifer

continued walking through the party and were

surprised when the mayor of Miami and his wife, April,

showed up.

"Mia, do you see this?" Jennifer asked her. "Is that

who I think it is?"

"Mayor Earl Roberson!" Mia announced while also

watching him and his wife as they were greeted by

Luther Simmons himself.

"What does the mayor have to do with Luther?" Jennifer asked as Sean suddenly appeared behind them out of nowhere, causing both girls to jump in surprise.

"Boy!" Mia cried, elbowing Sean in the mid-section. "Why do you always do that?"

"This is a really impressive turnout Luther has here," Sean said as he nodded across the room. "I see Luther knows some really important people like the Blackwell family."

"You know about them, Sean?" Mia asked.

"I've met Dante Blackwell a few times before," he admitted.

"I'm still trying to figure out how the mayor knows

Luther Simmons," Jennifer said while still watching

Mayor Roberson and Luther Simmons talking with

each other.

"Sean, has Luther told you anything yet?" Mia

asked him.

"I'll let Luther know what you said, Miss Moore,"

Sean suddenly said before leaning toward Jennifer's

cheek, kissing her quickly, and whispering something

into her ear before walking off.

Jennifer heard exactly what Sean just told her. She

then glanced to her right and saw Frank and two other

men a few feet away watching them. She discreetly

whispered loud enough over to Mia that they were

being watched.

FOUR

Three days after the dinner party at Luther Simmons's mansion, Sean and Jennifer met with Luther and Mia at the private airstrip and saw Luther's Rolls-Royce parked out beside Luther's private jet. Sean parked his Bentley beside the Rolls and was climbing out of the car just in time to see Frank and four of Luther's men on the security team climb out of the jet and head toward the Bentley.

"Mr. Carter," Frank stated as he walked to the car. He then spoke to Jennifer before addressing Sean again. "Mr. Simmons awaits your arrival on the jet."

"Thanks," Sean replied as he took Jennifer's hand

and saw that security had already taken his and Jennifer's luggage from the car and carried it to the jet.

Sean allowed Jennifer onto the jet first, but stepped on directly behind her. He then paused at the sight of Luther and Mia kissing on a sofa at the back of the jet.

"Hey, guys." Jennifer interrupted the kissing between Mia and Luther.

"Sean! Jennifer!" Luther called out with a smile as he stood up from beside Mia to greet the two. "I was beginning to wonder if the both of you were still coming or not."

"I always keep my word!" Sean said as he took a seat at the table with Luther sitting down across from him.

After leaving Sean and Luther to talk, Jennifer walked over to where Mia was sitting and staring at Sean, who was blankly ignoring her.

"You wanna tell me what the hell that was I walked in on just now, Mia?"

"Jennifer, it was just a kiss!"

"It looked like you two were close to having sex if I hadn't announced that Sean and I were on the damn plane with y'all!"

"Jennifer, you're thinking too much into it. I only allowed him to kiss me."

"Correct me if I'm wrong," Jennifer began, "but didn't I see him release your left titty when I cleared my throat, Mia."

Mia was unable to say anything in her defense and simply shook her head.

"Sean saw that, didn't he?"

Jennifer laughed as she shook her head at Mia.

"You're really pushing your luck, Mia. You know Sean saw exactly what I saw. Why do you think he's ignoring you?"

"I'm just doing my job, Jennifer."

"Which is why I think Sean didn't break Luther's neck when he got on the plane and saw you two about to have sex."

"We weren't having sex!"

"Yes!" Jennifer stated, just as she and Mia looked up as Luther reappeared.

"Excuse me, ladies. But, Jennifer, I'm to tell you that Sean is waiting for your return. He would like to talk to you."

Jennifer looked back at Mia before standing up from her seat. She then walked back over to where Sean was sitting and sat down beside him.

"Sean, you okay?"

"I'm good," he answered. "Luther's meeting friends in Costa Rica, so we're not the only ones going on this trip with him."

"He say who these friends were?"

"Just business friends," Sean replied.

Sean got comfortable and reached up and pulled down the flip-out screen that instantly turned on once it was open, showing a selection of movies from which

to choose.

~ ~ ~

Mia was ignored the entire flight from Florida to

Costa Rica. She attempted to try to talk to Sean twice

on the plane, but he ignored her both times or he woke

up Luther at one point after the drug lord had fallen

asleep. She gave up trying and decided to try again once

the jet landed and they were in Central America.

Mia allowed Luther to lead her off the jet by

holding her hand after the jet touched down. Mia was

shocked at how beautiful it was, never having visited

the country before.

"I take it you like what you're seeing?" Luther

asked, smiling as he stood watching Mia take in the scenery.

Mia shook her head in disbelief at how beautiful it was, and they were only on the landing strip. Mia followed alongside Luther and noticed that he was leading them over to a stretch Mercedes limousine that sat waiting on them.

Once the four of them were inside the limo and the security team placed their luggage into the Escalade parked behind the limo, Luther and Mia got into the limo first, followed by Sean and Jennifer.

"Jennifer!" Luther said, getting her attention. "Is this your first time to Costa Rica?"

"It is!" she answered as she looked back out of her

window as the limo began pulling off.

"I guess you and Tiffany are both seeing this place for the first time then," Luther stated with a smile as he wrapped Mia in his arms. "This should be enjoyable."

Mia could feel Sean's eyes burning into her, so she turned to look at him. She met his gray eyes that were darker than they normally were. She could see the anger where there was normally calm.

~ ~ ~

They arrived at a cottage twenty minutes after leaving the airstrip. Luther and Mia began walking toward the cottage while Jennifer took Sean by the hand and began leading him past the cottage and out onto the sand, only to begin walking along the water line on the beach.

"Sean, you okay?" Jennifer asked after a few quiet moments. "You've been extremely quiet the whole drive here and most of the plane ride down here."

"I'm good, Jennifer," Sean answered.

Expecting him to say more, and looking over at him when he didn't, Jennifer asked, "It's bothering you the way Mia's acting with Luther, isn't it?"

"Not really!" he replied. "This whole thing just reminds me of things between me and this woman I was seeing two years ago, that's all!"

"What happened?" Jennifer wanted to know.

Sean looked over at Jennifer and met her eyes. He

found himself opening up and telling her a part of his

personal life that not even his family knew.

~ ~ ~

Mia walked out to the back of the cottage while

Luther was on the phone making a call. She walked out

onto the sand and looked around for Sean and Jennifer,

spotting them a ways away. They were standing on the

water's edge with Sean's arms around Jennifer's

shoulders as she leaned in against him with both arms

wrapped around his waist. She instantly felt the strong

pull of jealousy, seeing how close Jennifer seemed to

be getting with Sean.

"You find Sean and Jennifer?" Luther asked as he

walked up behind Mia and wrapped his arms around

her from the back.

"They're right there." Mia nodded as Luther then began kissing on her neck and then cupping her right breast. She slowly pulled out of his embrace only to turn to face him and ask, "Who was that you called, Luther?"

"Friends," he answered.

"It sounded like another woman," Mia told him, faking jealousy.

Luther smiled as he pulled Mia back up against him.

He then kissed her and said, "The woman that's here with me is the only woman that's important to me, Tiffany. That was just friends of mine who are coming to the cottage for a visit. You'll meet them when they

get here."

Mia nodded her head and accepted the answer that

Luther had given her, but she made the mistake of

allowing him to kiss her again.

"There are two bedrooms inside, Luther."

She broke the kiss just in time to see Jennifer and

Sean walk past them, but she caught the look Sean shot

her before he and Jennifer entered the cottage. Mia

shook her head, realizing that the trip had started off

poorly.

~ ~ ~

Sean and Luther were talking behind the house

when Mia called out to let Luther know that his guests

had arrived. Sean and Luther walked back inside through the sliding glass door, where Luther broke out into a smile when he saw Captain Sinclair and his wife, Janice.

"Chris!" Luther called out, walking over and shaking hands with the captain. "It's good to see you."

"You as well, Luther," Captain Sinclair replied with a smile.

"Luther, aren't you forgetting someone?" Janice spoke up, drawing the attention of both Luther and her husband.

"Janice, how could I forget you?" Luther said as he walked over and hugged the extremely flirtatious white woman who had been after him since he began doing business with the captain.

Luther first introduced Sean and then Mia as

Tiffany, since that was what he knew her by, and then

Jennifer as Sean's girlfriend. Luther asked the women

if they minded if he spoke with Chris and Sean in

private.

"It better not be long, Luther!" Janice told him as

Luther, her husband, and Sean headed out the sliding

glass door and to the back of the cottage.

~ ~ ~

Sean was unsure why he was even invited outside

with Luther and the captain, but he stood silently as the

two men spoke with each other discussing names and

dates. Sean quickly put together that Captain Sinclair

was actually working with Luther on getting his heroin shipments in without any trouble from the Coast Guard or any other law enforcement. He was surprised to hear that Luther was paying the captain the type of money he was for ensuring that all his shipments made it into the docks when they were supposed to.

Once the discussion was over and both Luther and Chris started back inside, Sean found himself wondering exactly who Paul Smith was and why the name sounded familiar to him when he overheard it mentioned.

~ ~ ~

Sean went out to eat with the captain and his wife and then out to an outdoor bar with live entertainment that Luther had taken them to. Sean never got the

chance to talk with Jennifer and Mia together or with

Mia alone, since Luther kept her close. Instead, he took

Jennifer out onto the dance floor and while slow music

was playing, they danced together as he broke down

everything to her about the conversation between

Luther and Captain Sinclair.

"So Sinclair is working with Luther to get the drugs

into the state, huh?" Jennifer reiterated as a few

thoughts ran through her mind. "Did he say when the

next shipment is supposed to come in, Sean?"

"That wasn't mentioned," he told her. "Luther did

mention the name Paul Smith, though. The name

sounds familiar, but I can't remember where I

recognize it from, Jennifer."

"Sean, think about it!" she said, her eyes showing her excitement. "Paul Smith is chief Paul Smith of the Miami PD. We met him the night that guy you called came and got you and your cousin, Antonio, out of jail."

"Shit!" Sean remembered, laughing just as Mia appeared at his and Jennifer's side.

"Umm, excuse me," Mia said with an attitude. "Luther is taking us to this club a little ways from here. He wants to know if you two are ready or not?"

"You guys go ahead," Jennifer answered quickly. "Keep Luther busy, Mia. Sean and I are going back to the cottage to have a look around to see what we can find."

"Back to the cottage, huh?" Mia repeated as she cut her eyes off to Sean before saying, "Y'all hurry up. I'm not sure how long or what Luther's plans are."

"You know the number at the cottage, right?" Jennifer asked her.

"Of course!"

"Call when you're on your way back and let us know," Jennifer explained.

She then pointed out that Luther was making his way over to them on the dance floor.

~ ~ ~

Sean and Jennifer took a taxi back to the cottage after Luther, Mia, Chris, and Janice had left the bar.

The two rode back to the cottage in silence, both deep in their own thoughts. Jennifer never even realized when the taxi pulled up in front of the cottage, until Sean broke her out of her train of thought.

They paid the taxi driver and then walked up to the front door. Once they walked inside, Jennifer turned on the kitchen light.

"Keep most of the lights out!" Sean suddenly told her. "Just in case Mia can't call and warn us and Luther comes straight back here. I wanna be able to see him approaching, not the other way around."

Jennifer understood and agreed with Sean. She started for Luther's room as Sean went in his own direction inside the cottage.

Once Jennifer was in Luther's room, she went straight for his luggage. She pulled both pieces out and onto the bed. She began searching through them after she got them open, and found a brown envelope inside the second piece.

"Jesus!" she said in a whisper to herself after seeing the envelope was filled with nothing but $100s.

She was pulling the money from the envelope when a huge and strong hand wrapped around her mouth from the back, and she was lifted from her feet.

She was screaming behind the hand and fidgeting as best she could to get free from the strong arms that were holding her. Jennifer threw her legs up just as she was being carried out of the room, only to kick as hard as she could against the wall and push backward a little.

She screamed again behind the huge hand that stayed over her mouth. Once the person holding her turned and began backing out of the room while Jennifer continued fighting to get free, she heard a grunt-like sound, and then she was being taken down fast toward the ground.

Jennifer hit the floor and rolled around before she jumped to her feet in an attempt to defend herself, only to pause, stare at Sean, and fight with Luther's head of security.

Jennifer was frozen in place staring in complete shock and surprise upon seeing how Sean was fighting against Frank, who was taller and had to outweigh Sean by at least thirty or more pounds. She jumped at the sound of Frank's left leg being broken and heard Frank scream out in pain, right before Sean stepped into a spinning back kick that sent Frank's wide, big body falling backward onto his broken leg. He was knocked out before his head touched the floor.

~ ~ ~

Sean turned his attention to Jennifer after dealing with Frank, who was unconscious at the moment. He walked over to her and lightly brushed her hair out of her face.

"You okay?" he gently asked.

Jennifer nodded her head yes as she looked back at Frank and then back at Sean in disbelief. She could not find the words to express or explain what she was feeling or thinking as she stood there still staring at Sean.

"Jennifer, listen, I need you to focus for me," Sean told her firmly. "I'm going to take care of Frank's body, but I need you to go through the cottage and throw things around and make it look like someone was inside looking for something or trying to steal something. Trash the place, Jennifer!"

She nodded her head again to let Sean know that she understood, and watched him pick up Frank's heavy body and begin half-dragging and half-carrying him out of the cottage. Once Sean was gone, she got to work doing exactly what she was told. She began with the front area, trashing everything she laid her eyes on.

Jennifer remembered the money and rushed back into Luther's bedroom. She snatched up the envelope and the money. She stuffed the money back into the envelope and then hid it inside her bra before going about trashing Luther's room. She wanted to get to her and Sean's room next, that they were supposed to share.

FIVE

After immediately leaving Costa Rica, after getting a call from Sean that someone had broken into the cottage, even though he felt odd about the whole thing since he stayed there for years, Luther rode back to Florida in complete silence. He wondered what the hell had happened to Frank, since he knew that his head of security was on the trip with them, but was ordered to keep out of sight.

Once Luther was back at the airstrip in Miami, he asked Sean to see to Mia and get her home after explaining that he needed to handle something.

Once he got inside his Rolls, Luther went straight

for his phone. He pulled up the number of an old friend, thinking that he had new enemies. He sat and listened to the line ring once and then two more times before it was finally answered.

"Grant here."

"Grant, it's Luther."

"I'm aware of who it is, Luther. What can I do for you?"

"I may need your services. You still for hire?"

"Depends on what the numbers sound like, Luther!"

"How does $2 million sound to you, Grant?"

"Sounds like you're talking my kind of numbers. Now what can I do for you?"

"First, you can get your ass to Miami like now, and I'll explain the rest once you're here in front of me," Luther told him before hanging up on his friend and trying to call Frank's phone again, only to receive his voice mail again.

After hanging up the phone and dropping it onto the seat beside him, Luther sat down and stared out the car window trying to understand what the hell was really going on.

~ ~ ~

Sean got Jennifer home first, only to end up sitting at her apartment longer than any of them had planned. He stood at the front door with the porch light off, listening as Jennifer broke down everything that she and he found out about Luther and his business associates. Sean was deep in his own thoughts when he heard Mia yell out his name, which broke his train of thought.

"Yeah, Mia!" he answered, turning his head to look at her.

"Didn't you just hear what I asked you?" Mia questioned him with an attitude.

"If I had, I would have answered you!" Sean told her. "How about repeating yourself, Mia?"

"You know what!" Mia said, sucking her teeth as she shot up out of her seat and walked over to Sean. She grabbed his arm and snatched him around to face her. "I'm so sick of your attitude. If you got something on your chest, then you need to get it off!"

Sean held Mia's eyes for a few moments before shaking his head and smirking at her.

He then shifted his eyes to look at Jennifer and said, "Jennifer, just call me when you got a plan. I'll see you later."

"What?" Mia yelled, grabbing at his arm again, only to hear Jennifer yell her name. She looked back at Jennifer and saw her partner shake her head.

"Just let him go, Mia!" Jennifer told her best friend, after seeing the anger and hurt in Mia's eyes. "Talk to him later after you both calm down a little bit."

Mia turned her attention back to Sean and watched him walk back out to his car. She slammed the door once he was inside the Bentley and was pulling off.

~ ~ ~

Sean headed nowhere but still drove around after leaving Jennifer's place. He drove around for more than three hours until he realized that he was back in Jacksonville, where he pulled up in front of his mentor's house, where he saw Henry's pickup truck out in the driveway.

He parked his Bentley and climbed out, only to hear a very faint sound. Sean was already ducking and spinning on the balls of his feet while pulling out his Ruger. He came up swinging the gun at the same time a chrome Desert Eagle was aimed directly at his face.

"You're getting sloppy, son," Henry stated while

still holding the hand canon aimed at Sean. "You let me get this close up on you with a thing like this?"

After lowering his Ruger, Sean explained, "I got a lot on my mind, Henry."

"A lot on your mind, huh?" Henry repeated with a short laugh. "Keep moving like you just did, and ya won't have a mind to have shit on, son!"

Upon hearing his mentor and refusing to fight with him, Sean followed Henry up to the house and walked inside to a dimly lit front room, which was not a surprise to him.

"Sit down, son," Henry told Sean, pointing to a spot on the sofa across from him as he sat on his favorite chair. "So, what's this woman's name, Sean?"

Sean was not surprised that Henry had figured him out as fast as he had, since the old white man knew him better than most. Sean sighed deeply as he fell back into his seat and began to explain to his mentor what was going on.

~ ~ ~

Mia was stressed out from everything that was going on, from the case she was working on against Luther Simmons to her feelings for Sean and the jealousy she was feeling about Sean and Jennifer's new friendship and how close they were becoming. She sat in her dark den back at her apartment twenty minutes after Jennifer had dropped her off. She sat trying to put together everything in her headfirst concerning the case, while blocking out her relationship problems with Sean.

She unfolded her legs from underneath her and turned on the lamp beside the sofa. Mia then picked up the pen and writing pad that she had left on the coffee table and began writing down names connected with Luther Simmons, starting with the Gambainos and ending with captain Chris Sinclair.

Mia remembered the mayor when he showed up at Luther's dinner party, so she wrote down mayor Earl Roberson and put a question mark beside his name, since nothing was completely sure about the mayor.

Mia stared at the list and played things out in her mind. She wanted to really nail this whole case. She then picked up her phone and called Luther's number, only to have the phone company explain that the number she was calling was no longer in service.

"What the hell?" Mia said confused, trying the number again only to hear the same message. "What the hell is going on?"

She called Sean's number next and got his voice message, which caused her to suck her teeth and call Jennifer.

"Hello," Jennifer answered in the middle of the third ring.

"Jennifer, it's me. You sleeping?"

"I wish I could sleep. What's up, Mia?"

"I need you to call Sean on a three-way for me. His

ass isn't answering my calls now."

"You two need to stop this mess! Hold on, Mia!"

Mia sucked her teeth while thinking Sean needed

to man up and talk to her. She heard the line suddenly

begin to ring right before Jennifer's voice came back

onto the line.

"Mia, you there?"

"Yeah, I'm here."

"Yeah!" Sean finally answered after three rings.

"What's up, Jennifer, or should I be asking Mia what

she wants since she just called?"

"You know what? Whatever, Sean! Look, I just

need you to look into things with Mayor Roberson.

Find out if he's connected to Luther as well. We got

the chief and the captain, but we need to know if the mayor is a part of the group as well. Can you do that, please?"

"I'll let you know what I can find," Sean replied before he then called out to Jennifer.

"Yeah, Sean? What's up?" Jennifer answered him.

"Listen, I've been thinking about something and I want your opinion on it. I'ma call you tomorrow after I handle something first."

After hearing Sean hang up the phone after talking directly to Jennifer, Mia heard herself say out loud, "Oooh, his ass makes me sick!"

~ ~ ~

Sean finally got back to his own place long enough

to shower and change into his normal gear of black

jeans, a wife beater, and his brown Tims. He grabbed

his burner, keys, and cell phone before he snatched up

his black leather jacket from behind the bedroom door.

He locked up his condo and took the elevator back

down to the lobby. Sean then walked out the front

door as he was calling his cousin's phone.

"Who this?" Tony answered, sounding half asleep.

"This is Sean. I need to holla at you real quick,

Cousin."

"I'm listening. What up, Cuz?"

Sean explained what he needed from Tony and

how much he was willing to pay to get both problems

handled. He then explained that he was on his way over

to Tony's apartment.

"Let me hit up a few people," Tony told his cousin.

"But I'ma be ready when you get here though."

Sean hung up with Tony after handling one issue, and then he called the number to the friend that Henry had told him to call, explaining to the friend who was actually waiting on his call what he needed done. He then ended that call once a price was agreed on for the work.

SIX

Jennifer was up earlier than she expected she would be, considering what time she finally got to lay down to sleep. She joined Mia as the two of them met with their boss to inform him on the latest update with the case and all that they had gathered so far. Jennifer explained that they were looking deeper into finding not only a connection with the mayor and Luther Simmons if there indeed was one, but also trying to pin down each party to the exact crime for which they were a part.

After their meeting was finished and Jennifer and Mia left, they stopped to eat a late breakfast at an

IHOP they came upon. Jennifer held up her hand for Mia to wait as she dug out her ringing cell phone.

"It's Sean," she stated before answering his call. "Hello."

Jennifer and Sean were on the phone for about eight minutes, with her telling him where she was and then where she was going afterward. Jennifer hung up the phone and looked at Mia.

"We gotta finish up fast, Mia. I gotta meet Sean back at my place in an hour."

"Meet Sean at your place in an hour for what?" Mia asked, her face balled up as she followed alongside Jennifer as the two of them continued toward the IHOP entrance.

"Mia, you were on the phone last night when Sean said he needed my help with something," Jennifer told her friend as the two of them entered the restaurant.

After the two women were escorted to a table by a hostess, they sat across from each other. But once the hostess placed menus in front of them and walked away, Mia bluntly asked, "What's going on between you and Sean, Jennifer?"

"Excuse me?" Jennifer asked, staring at her friend with a look of disbelief. "Did you just really ask me that, Mia?"

"Answer the question!"

Jennifer shook her head and laughed before saying, "I don't know what's wrong with you, but to answer your question, there's nothing going on between Sean

and me. If you would just open your eyes you'll see that

that boy is in love with you. But you're so caught up in

acting like you're really a drug lord's girlfriend that

you've lost all respect for Sean by kissing and allowing

Luther to feel all over you. I'm surprised Sean is still

helping us, let alone allowing Luther to still breathe.

Maybe you need to re-evaluate yourself and your

relationship with Sean, Mia."

Jennifer changed her mind about breakfast with

Mia and decided to pick up something she could eat on

the way home. She picked up her things, stood up from

the table, and left Mia right where she was sitting.

~ ~ ~

Jennifer made it back to her place a little while later, after she stopped to pick up food at a restaurant she spotted on her way home. She got inside the apartment and got herself together before calling Sean back to let him know that she was home.

She focused on her food after hanging up with Sean. Jennifer then ate and watched the television, when her doorbell sounded off throughout the apartment.

Jennifer set down the Styrofoam plate of food and walked to her front door. After she peeked out the hole to see who was there, she unlocked and then opened the door, only to turn and head back into her den. Once she stepped inside, she picked up her food and began eating, just as Mia walked into the room and dropped down onto the sofa beside her.

"I'm sorry!" Mia apologized, staring at Jennifer. "I guess I'm really not acting myself, and I admit that I am really trying extra hard to take down Luther Simmons, and I really am in love with Sean. I just will be happy when this case is over with."

"Well truthfully, I don't think we're anywhere close to closing this case, Mia," Jennifer admitted. "I think we've only found a few major players on the team. I truly feel that Luther is playing with a full deck and has some real power plays that we're up against."

"I agree!" Mia said. "But I think the main thing we've got going great for us is—!"

"Sean!" Jennifer finished for Mia, causing her friend and partner to smile while nodding her head in agreement.

~ ~ ~

Sean stood outside the warehouse where Tony and Hulk had brought him. He was leaning on the front of Tony's ride listening to his cousin tell him how business had been going so far since he was introduced to Michael Brown. Sean glanced at his wrist and saw that it was 12:15 p.m.

"Yo, Sean!" Hulk said, tapping Sean on the arm to get his attention. "Ain't that ya ride right there, fam?"

Sean shifted his gaze and spotted the new BMW 650i he recently bought after selling the Bentley. He slowly smiled when he saw the black-on-black matte

sports car as it was driven around to the front of the

warehouse and parked in front of him, Tony, and Hulk.

"Damn, this bitch is bad!" Rick cried out, smiling

after climbing out of the car and looking over at Sean.

"Bruh, you got me wanting to cash in and get me one

of these futuristic muthafuckers, my nigga! This bitch

is bad!"

Sean was still smiling when he walked over to the

car and slowly ran his hand along the edge, taking in

the whole black-on-black color scheme that matched

his Bentley. He also had the windows tinted as black as

they could get, making it impossible to see inside but

easy to see out. Sean walked around to the driver's side

where Tony's friend Rick stood waiting.

"Bruh, let me give you the rundown of what the fuck I put in this muthafucker!" Rick told Sean, stepping back and allowing him to climb into the car onto the black leather seats.

He went on to tell Sean about all the different compartments he installed inside the BMW 650i, and even about the case he had built specially some time ago that fit inside the trunk and could hold some serious heavy-powered shit back there.

Sean nodded his head in approval, but looked back up at Rick and said, "Hold on to the number I gave you. I'ma be contacting you again real soon."

Sean left the warehouse and followed behind Hulk

and Tony back to Overtown. He then pulled up in front of Tony's drop spot and saw T.J., Nina, and her sister, Maria, out front. He parked the i8 behind T.J.'s Crown Vic and climbed out.

"God damn!" T.J. yelled, smiling after seeing Sean step out of his new BMW 650i. "Fam, what's really up? You change rides like a nigga like me changes his shoes. What happened to the Bentley?"

"Changed up!" Sean replied, looking over at Nina to catch her staring at him, before she quickly looked away when they locked eyes.

"Yo, T.J.," Tony called out as he and Hulk walked up on him and Sean. "Where's what I told you to put up for Sean?"

"It's in the spot!" T.J. replied, nodding back at the apartment.

Tony nodded his head in return, looked at Sean, and said, "Cuz, come on. Let's see what type of toys my boy Bam sent over here for us to play with."

~ ~ ~

Sean finally made it across town to Jennifer's apartment after finishing up with his cousin, only to see Mia's car parked out in front of Jennifer's spot. Sean parked the i8 behind Mia's ride and then pulled out his phone and called Jennifer.

"Hello!"

"Jennifer, I'm outside."

"You coming in?"

"I can't right now! I gotta handle something with Luther, but I need you to come out here real quick so I can go."

After hanging up with Jennifer after she said she was on her way outside, Sean waited and leaned against his car with his arms folded across his chest, just as he heard his name. He looked to his right and saw Jennifer heading toward him.

"Hey you!" she greeted, hugging Sean once she walked up onto him. "You do know that Mia's inside, right?"

"I saw her car there!" he said, nodding toward Mia's ride, before he quickly changed the subject. "But I need your help with something here."

"What's up?" she asked, watching him pull out something from his pocket and hand it over to her.

"What's this?"

"Look at both of these pictures and tell me which one you think I should get?" he asked, watching her facial expression as she looked down at the two photos.

She was confused for a few moments as to why Sean had her look at two photos of the same yet slightly different item. She caught on at the last moment, looking at Sean with a questioning look.

"Sean, is this what I think it is?"

Sean nodded his head and said, "Yes! So which one do you think is best?"

Jennifer smiled as she looked back at the photos.

She then handed him the picture she thought was the best choice.

"This one?" he asked, smiling down at her.

"I'm sure of it!" Jennifer answered with a smile.

Sean thanked Jennifer and gave her a hug, receiving a kiss to the cheek in return. He told her to call him if she needed him as he climbed into his new i8. He started up the BMW and backed out of the parking lot. Just as he was pulling off, he caught sight of Mia standing at the corner of Jennifer's apartment building staring at him drive away.

~ ~ ~

Sean was still thinking about his plans and the excitement he saw on Jennifer's face when he showed her the two pictures and let her decide which photo was best, when he arrived and pulled up to Luther's mansion. He saw four armed security guards, none of whom he recognized.

"Open the gate," he yelled out the window at the non-moving nor responding security detail. He yelled again for them to open up the gate. After getting no response from any of the men, he opened up the car door and climbed out, causing all four of them to draw their weapons and aim directly at him.

He laughed lightly at what was happening in front of him and held up his hands as if he was surrendering. He even turned and attempted to climb back into his car, only to spin back toward his right, away from the car, as he pulled out his Ruger and dropped into a squat

position. He pulled the trigger of the Ruger four times.

Boom! Boom! Boom! Boom!

Sean dropped all four armed guards, hitting them

each in the legs instead of killing them. He got the gates

open himself and then got back into the car, leaving all

four guards laid out in front of Luther's front gate.

Sean saw Luther with a brown-skinned man

dressed in a dark suit, but he noticed the team of armed

security that were now holding nothing smaller than

AR-15s aimed at the BMW. Sean parked his 650i

beside Luther's Rolls-Royce and climbed from the car.

"Who's the new guy?" Sean asked as he boldly

made his way through the team of armed killers to stop

in front Luther.

"Sean, this is Peter Grant," Luther introduced, nodding to the guy beside him. "He's my new head of security."

Sean paid the guy no attention and said, "You may wanna get some medical attention for the four out at the front gate!"

Luther shook his head and smiled before he turned and re-entered the mansion, with Grant and Sean following right behind him. He walked into the sitting room and took a seat as Sean sat down across from him while Grant positioned himself at the entrance of the room.

"So, I take it Frank never showed back up from

Costa Rica?" Sean asked with a shake of his head before he nodded to the new guy and asked, "He any better than the last one?"

"Actually, Sean, Grant is a retired Special Forces sergeant and has one of the best-known security firms in Florida," Luther explained.

"Never heard of 'im," Sean replied. "So what's up? What you want to talk to me about?"

"There's a dinner banquet that's being held tonight and I'm invited," Luther explained. "I need you ready and here by 7:15 p.m. tonight. You'll ride with us!"

"Us?"

"Grant and myself, Sean!"

"So the sergeant's going, too, huh?" Sean asked,

shifting his eyes over to the new guy and smirking.

"Yeah, all right! I'll be here by 7:15 p.m."

"You're leaving?" Luther asked after seeing Sean quickly stand to his feet.

"Yeah!" he replied as he passed the sergeant. Sean looked back at Luther and said, "I gotta handle something important."

~ ~ ~

"I don't like that kid, Luther," Grant stated as soon as Sean walked out of the house. "He's not only cocky, but there's just something about that boy that just doesn't sit right with me."

Luther chuckled lightly after listening to Grant before he replied, "I'll admit it, Grant, Sean is pretty cocky, but he's a solid guy. He's come through for me

more than a few times, so just trust him."

"Yeah, I hear you," Grant answered, following

Luther from the sitting room.

But Grant had already made the decision that he

would be keeping a real close eye on Sean Carter.

SEVEN

Mia was surprised when she received a call from Luther Simmons asking her to attend some type of award banquet to which he was invited. She got herself ready and dressed in an Oscar de la Renta gown that was sent to her by Luther, which even had a white diamond necklace that was part of the whole ensemble.

She was doing something with her hair, since she was caught off guard by the invitation, but Mia was all ready by the time the Rolls-Royce showed up and Luther greeted her at her second apartment's front door.

"You look beautiful," Luther told her, smiling as he looked Mia over in the gown that he had bought for her. "You ready to go?"

"Just let me grab my purse," she told him as she walked away to pick up her handbag from the coffee table inside the den.

She returned to the front door and followed Luther outside. She then locked up the front door and started out to the car. However, she paused once her eyes landed on Sean dressed in a black designer suit and black silk dress shirt that was unbuttoned at the neck.

"Everything okay?" Mia heard someone ask, snapping her out of her stare. She looked at Luther and put on a smile. "Yes, I'm fine!"

Mia continued walking toward the Rolls-Royce while trying not to stare at Sean as she passed him to climb into the back of the car. Mia then moved over to the far left of the back seat of the Rolls as Luther climbed inside beside her.

"Who's he?" Mia asked, nodding to the guy that was up front behind the steering wheel.

"He's my new head of security," Luther answered as Sean sat up front beside Grant.

Once the Rolls pulled off, Mia turned to Luther and asked, "So what's this award you're supposed to be receiving?"

"Actually, I'm not really sure!" Luther told her. "I was told by a friend that I would be receiving an award tonight, so I wanted to have the most gorgeous woman

I know there on my arm."

Mia accepted a kiss from Luther, but she was not

surprised to see Sean staring back at her through the

rearview mirror. Mia mouthed the words, "I love you,"

to Sean as he sat staring at her, only to have him look

away and say nothing in return.

~ ~ ~

They arrived at the banquet hall and saw the line of

cars and limousines. Grant slowly made his way to the

front of the hall, just as a parking attendant rushed out

to the car. He quickly climbed out to see the young

bodyguard open the back door for Luther and his date

to exit.

"Thank you!" Mia replied, addressing her thanks to Sean, who simply nodded his head before closing the car door behind her.

They entered the hall to see that it was packed with well-dressed businessmen and well-known politicians and their dates or wives. Mia followed alongside Luther as they slowly made their way through the crowd, with Luther being stopped every few minutes by someone who knew him or wanted to talk to him.

"I'm glad to see you made it," Luther and Mia heard someone say, just as they reached their assigned table. The both of them looked up to see Mayor Eberson and his wife.

"Mayor Eberson!" Luther said, smiling as he shook

hands with the man. He then addressed his wife before directing his attention back to the mayor and said, "Why wouldn't I come, Eberson? Anytime someone wants to give me an award, I'm always willing to accept it."

Mia stood by Luther's side while he stood talking with the mayor for a few more minutes. She looked around in search of Sean but only saw the new head of security not far away. But Sean appeared to be nowhere in the building.

"Tiffany," Luther called out to get her attention as he motioned to the chair that he had pulled out for her.

Once the two of them were seated at the table and the band continued playing, Mia was still looking around for Sean, when Luther called out to someone.

She looked up after somewhat recognizing the name, just as a familiar face walked up to the table to greet Luther.

"Chief Smith!" Luther said as he and the chief shook hands. "You don't know my date, Tiffany Moore."

"Hello, Miss—!" he began, before he then paused and stared at Mia with an odd look on his face. "Haven't we met before somewhere, Miss Moore?"

"I doubt it, Chief!" Mia replied with a smile. "I'm sure I would remember someone as handsome as you."

Mia got the chief to smile and then turned her attention back to Luther. She felt her heart beating fast, and she realized that at any moment her cover could be blown, since she remembered the chief perfectly well from the night she introduced herself as Agent Mia Washington.

Once the chief returned to his table a few feet away where his wife was seated, Mia caught him looking back at her with the same odd look on his face.

"Luther!" Mia whispered into his ear. "I need to use the ladies' room. I'll be right back."

After leaving the table to make her way through the crowd, Mia rushed to the back of the banquet hall and saw a sign for the restrooms. As she was rushing up the hallway, she felt a strong and solid grip grab onto her arm; and before she knew it, she was snatched into a dark room off to her right.

"Mia, relax!"

Mia recognized the voice just as the room was lit up by a cell phone that showed Sean's face. She fell into him and wrapped her arms around him as she lay her head onto his chest.

"Sean, we got a problem!"

"Relax!" he repeated as he ran his hand through her hair. "I already know! I saw the chief with Luther after you left the table. I'm pretty sure he remembered who you are, because he watched you while you were leaving the table."

"I need to get out of here, Sean!"

"I'm already on it!" Sean told her.

He then explained that he called Jennifer and his cousin to meet them on the corner in twenty minutes.

"In twenty minutes?" Mia cried out, only for Sean to tell her to keep it down. She lowered her voice and said, "Why do we need that long to get out of this place?"

"Because, when I was following you back here, I saw Luther call over the new head of security. It's gonna be fun, but a little difficult getting away from here. You holding?"

"In this gown, Sean?" Mia asked sarcastically.

He pulled out the Glock 19 from his back holster that was a part of the specially made double shoulder holster that held guns across the back instead of the sides.

He then handed Mia his Glock and asked, "You do know how to use this, right?"

"Really, Sean?" Mia said, shooting him a look as she checked the magazine to make sure the clip was fully loaded.

While Mia did her check, Sean waited until she was finished and then shut off his phone light and cracked open the closet door to see that the hallway was clear. He then motioned her out of the closet.

"Head straight for the exit behind us," Sean told her, staring up the hallway to make sure the halls remained clear.

Doing as she was told, she rushed down the hall

and headed toward the exit. Mia pushed open the exit door, which caused a loud alarm to go off. She looked back to see that Sean was gone, just as she was grabbed from the back with a hand over her mouth.

She reacted out of defense and stomped on the foot of her attacker, and then smashed her elbow back into his mid-section. She could hear the air get knocked out of him. She leaned forward as she tossed her attacker forward over her back.

"Quite impressive!" Grant stated as he got up from the ground onto his knees with a smile on his face. "So I understand that you're with the FBI and that your name isn't Tiffany Moore but Mia Washington."

"Look, Grant," Mia started at the same time she

caught the movement behind Luther's head of security.

"You're just now coming into the whole scene and really don't know what's going on. Just turn and walk away before you get too deep into all of this!"

"Mr. Simmons is waiting for you inside the—!"

Mia's eyes opened wide after Sean appeared clearly right behind the head of security. She watched as he swiftly and easily broke Grant's neck, only to let his body drop lifelessly to the ground before holding his hand out to her.

"Mia, come on!" Sean called out to her, seeing the way she was staring at him.

She immediately snapped out of the state she was in and took Sean's hand, allowing him to lead her out from the back alleyway behind the banquet hall. She

stared over at three other men who all lay on the

ground just as Grant had behind them.

"You did that too, didn't you?"

Sean heard Mia but chose not to bother to respond

to her at the moment. Instead, he led her out to the

sidewalk where he saw Luther's Rolls-Royce parked in

front of the banquet hall.

They made it out to the street corner where they

saw Jennifer, before Sean spotted his cousin and what

looked like twenty men ready to light up the streets.

Sean then took Mia straight over to her partner and

yelled up the street to his cousin, Tony.

"Sean, what are you doing?" Mia asked as she

watched him take off his suit jacket and begin to pull off his shoulder holster and undo his dress shirt.

"I'm about to finish this tonight!" Sean answered as Tony, Nina, and T.J. walked up.

"Sean, wait and just listen to me!" Mia pleaded with him after seeing the bulletproof vest Nina had just handed him. "Please, just let us handle this another way. We've got enough evidence that can get Luther put behind bars long enough for us to run down on all of his associations. Just, please, let us handle this our way. Please, Sean!"

He stared straight into her eyes and saw the pleading there, but Sean looked at Jennifer and saw the questioning in her eyes.

He finally gave in and said, "All right. I'ma let you

two handle this your way, but if you two can't handle

it, then I'm handling it my way."

EIGHT

Luther expected it as soon as he heard the screams from the sirens approaching his home. He stood from the chair behind his office desk and made his way out into the upstairs hallway. He heard his front door when it came crashing in and heard the FBI announce their arrival.

As he made his way to the top of the staircase, he saw a team of FBI in full uniform rush upstairs straight at him, all holding assault rifles. Luther put up no type of fight as he was forcefully slammed to the floor and handcuffed behind his back.

"Luther Simmons, you're under arrest and have the

right to remain silent—!"

He recognized the voice as he was read his rights.

Luther then looked up into the eyes of Mia Washington, who he only knew as Tiffany Moore.

He chuckled after he was pulled up to his feet as he continued staring at Mia while being escorted downstairs.

"Mia Washington! Agent Mia Washington!"

Luther continued repeating Mia's name even as he was escorted out the front door of his mansion. He then pulled against the hold that held onto his arms as he was being placed into the back of an FBI truck.

"Gimme a second! I wanna say something to Agent Washington."

Mia nodded her head to the two escorting agents and looked back at Luther and said, "What is it, Luther? What do you want?"

"So all this time you were an FBI agent, huh?" he questioned. "You do know all of this is a waste of time, right? You do know that none of this was worth the time because neither you nor the FBI bullshit has anything on me, and my team of attorneys will have me out in weeks."

"We'll see about that!" Luther heard someone say as he looked to his left and was surprised and then shocked to see Jennifer Lewis dressed in an FBI vest as well.

"What the hell!" Luther said in confusion as he

stared from Jennifer back to Mia. "You two are both with the FBI?"

"We got you, Luther!" Jennifer replied with a big smile as she told the escorting agents to place Luther Simmons in the back of the truck.

Jennifer could only shake her head as she looked away from the truck to see Mia still staring at it with a look on her face.

Jennifer stepped closer to Mia and asked, "Mia, what's wrong?"

"He's right, Jennifer!" Mia expressed. "We really don't have enough to hold him, and I'm sure he'll be out as soon as we get him locked up! I can't live with that, Jennifer."

"Mia, come on! We'll get him!" Jennifer promised

her partner. "We've got the police captain and chief as

well as the mayor. We'll get them, Mia!"

Mia wanted to believe her friend and partner, but

she knew different. Mia followed alongside Jennifer

deep in thought as the two of them walked over to their

car and headed back to headquarters to report to their

boss.

~ ~ ~

Mia and Jennifer were at headquarters meeting

with special agent Aaron Davis. They were attending a

quick briefing on what they had and who was a part of

the entire investigation. Mia allowed Jennifer to take

the lead and provide Davis with the names of the

people in connection with the Luther Simmons investigation, including Mayor Eberson, chief Paul Smith, and captain Chris Sinclair.

After leaving the conference room, once the briefing was over, Mia really did not want to talk with anyone else. She rode the elevator down to the parking garage and was stepping off just as her phone began to ring.

She pulled out her phone and saw that Jennifer was calling.

"Yeah, Jennifer," Mia answered, even though she did not want to talk.

"Mia, where are you?"

"I'm heading home, Jennifer. What's up?"

Mia listened as her friend asked out of concern if she was okay. Jennifer wanted to know if Mia wanted her to come over. Mia explained that she was fine, but that she did not mind if Jennifer came by her apartment later that night.

After hanging up the phone with Jennifer and leaving the office, Mia started for home while thinking about Sean and the apartment she had been renting for the investigation. She picked up her phone and pulled up his number. She called him and drove while listening to the line ring until his voice message picked up.

She left a message for him to call her back once he had received the message. Mia hung up the phone and then dropped it into her center console, sighing as she

continued driving back to her place.

~ ~ ~

Mia was happy to hear about their first victory

seven days later, when Luther Simmons was denied

bail. But she took little joy in the small win and had a

good reason. A one month later, Luther made his first

appearance in court for a pre-trial that his attorneys put

a motion in for. They requested a dismissal due to lack

of evidence to which the judge denied again. However,

the judge did surprise both the state and FBI by

granting Luther bail at $2 million.

Mia and Jennifer dealt with the news reporters. The

two agents and Aaron Davis gave quick and short

interviews before leaving the courthouse.

"What now, sir?" Jennifer asked as she, Mia, and

Agent Davis walked off together after dealing with the

press. "We took a shot at Simmons, and even brought

in the mayor, chief, and captain, but we still lost

Simmons!"

"We'll figure this out some way," Agent Davis said

as he stopped at the back end of his car. "Luther

Simmons is gonna slip up, and when he does, it's his

ass, and we'll be there to pick up the pieces."

~ ~ ~

Luther bonded out two hours after receiving bail.

He was met at the exit of the jail by his lead attorney,

Anthony Wells.

"Did you take care of everything I asked you to?"

Luther asked his attorney as the two of them walked

out to his Rolls-Royce that sat curbside waiting.

"I made the calls, Mr. Simmons," Mr. Wells

informed Luther as he climbed into the back of the car

with his client. "Everyone was released a few hours

ago, and both Chief Smith and Mayor Eberson want

you to contact them as soon as possible."

Luther waved his hand dismissively at the

comment his attorney made about the mayor and chief.

Luther simply sat quietly for a few moments deep in

thought, putting a few things together inside his head

before speaking again and asking his attorney for his

cell phone.

After making a call from his attorney's phone, Luther listened to the line ring a few times, when it was answered by a woman who spoke Spanish.

Luther spoke in the best Spanish he knew and asked if José was around. He was placed on hold and waited a few minutes.

"Hola!" a man answered with a deep and thick Spanish accent.

"José, this is Luther. Can you speak?"

"Luther, my friend. Of course I can speak with you. What can I do for you? It's been a long time since we last spoke."

"José, are your brothers still in business?"

"Of course, my friend. Do you have some trouble

you want them to handle?"

"José, I need you to send both of your brothers here to the States. I will send you $4 million for their services. How does that sound to you?"

"They will be on the next plane to Florida, my friend."

Luther spent a few more minutes on the phone with José setting up everything for his brothers, Hector and Ortiz, for when they arrived to the state.

Luther hung up the phone and then looked over at his attorney and said, "I need you to set up a meeting with Captain Sinclair. Let him know that I need his help with something important. Tell him there's $150,000 in it for him!"

~ ~ ~

Three weeks after Luther Simmons was released, Mia continued to follow the case on the news and through Jennifer and her boss. She spent most of her time trying to contact Sean, who seemed to just somehow disappear from the scene, and she was unable to contact him. She tossed her cell phone down and was just getting to her feet when the doorbell sounded throughout her apartment.

She sighed as she started toward her front door. She thought Jennifer was stopping by to see her. Mia first checked the peephole and saw two guys outside her door, one white and the other black.

"Can I help you?" she called through the door.

"Ma'am, my name is detective Robert Robinson and I have my partner, detective Stanley Harris, with me. We were wondering if we could have a few words with you, if you don't mind, ma'am."

"Talk to me about what?"

"Ma'am, could we talk about this face-to-face?"

Mia rushed back into the other room and grabbed her cell phone. She immediately called 911 to check and see if Detectives Robinson and Harris were on the force. She kept up the conversation with the two detectives until she got the answer she needed that let her know she was, in fact, speaking with two real detectives.

"Just a second!" Mia called out, sliding her phone

into her pocket before unlocking and opening her front door. "What can I do for you, officers?"

Mia never saw the fist that came flying straight at her. Her head snapped back after the pain exploded in her face, right before she blacked out.

~ ~ ~

After waking up from the deep sleep she was in, Mia slowly opened her eyes, only for the pain to shoot through her nose and between her eyes. She tried reaching up to rub her nose, only to feel that her hands were cuffed behind her back. She focused her eyes as she began looking around and realized that she was in some type of room.

Mia heard voices and tried to hear what was being

said as well as where the voices were coming from. She

then realized the voices were coming from next to her

through the wall, but she caught Luther's name, which

made her realize she had been kidnapped.

She snapped her neck when she swung her head

around after hearing a door open. Mia found herself

staring at one of the same two detectives that had

shown up at her apartment.

"I see you finally woke up," Detective Harris said

when he spied Mia's open eyes. "You need to use the

bathroom?"

"Where am I?" Mia asked.

"Don't worry about where you're at! Do you need

to use the bathroom?"

"Why are you—? Wait!" Mia yelled as the detective

was closing the door. "I need to pee!"

The detective opened the door back up and walked

over to her to unlock the handcuffs she was wearing.

Mia was then escorted from the room and up a short

hallway until the detective stopped in front of a closed

door.

"There's the bathroom. You've got five minutes!"

Detective Harris told her as she positioned herself

against the wall in front of the bathroom door.

Mia was happy for the privacy as she entered the

bathroom and shut the door behind her. She saw there

was no lock inside, and there were no windows.

"I can't believe this shit!" Mia said as she undid her

jeans and began pushing them down to use the toilet.

She paused after feeling something familiar.

She quickly pulled her pants back up and saw the print of her cell phone inside her pocket. Mia dug out the phone and gave a silent thanks to God before turning it on.

She did not want to talk and be heard, so she sent a text message to Jennifer explaining what had happened. But she was unsure of where she was. Mia started to turn the phone off, but she thought there might be a chance to hear from Sean if she texted him as well.

~ ~ ~

Jennifer was shocked by the text message that she

had just received from Mia. She was up and out of her bed within seconds. She threw on a pair of jeans and a T-shirt while on the phone calling for backup to help her locate and rescue her partner.

She spoke with an agent at headquarters and demanded to speak with Special Agent Davis, only to find out that her boss had gone home for the night. Jennifer yelled at the agent on the phone and demanded to be connected with Special Agent Davis's phone.

She heard the connection die for a few moments before Agent Davis's voice came through the line. Jennifer wasted no time screaming about Mia's text message and not knowing where she had been taken.

Jennifer tried to stay calm listening to her boss and his FBI protocol bullshit. She could only take so much before she yelled at him to find her partner before she hung up the phone on him.

Jennifer was panicked and worried as she paced back and forth in front of her dining room table, trying to figure out what to do when she remembered something. She snatched her phone back up and pulled up a number she was given just in case of an extreme emergency. She called the number and found herself on the phone with some guy who had an accent she could not decipher.

"Who is this?" the voice asked.

"Umm, I was given this number by a friend of—!"

"Wait a minute, girl!" the voice cut her off.

While waiting a few minutes after the voice left the phone, Jennifer was starting to wonder if the call had ended, when a familiar voice came on the line.

"Jennifer, is that you?"

"Sean, it's Mia! We can't find her," Jennifer yelled as she burst into tears.

Jennifer heard Sean calling her name and trying to get her to calm down. She composed herself enough to tell him about Mia's message and explained that she didn't know where Mia was being held.

"I'ma call you back when I've got her," was all Sean said before he hung up the phone on her.

~ ~ ~

Mia was unsure exactly how long she was held inside the room. She could hear different sounds and sometimes new voices join in with the two voices that she recognized as Detectives Robinson and Harris. Mia had to use the bathroom again, and she was also hungry as hell. She wanted to try her phone again and see if Jennifer had received her message or not.

She heard the door open and looked up to see Detective Harris enter the room carrying a Burger King bag and drink. Mia sat there just staring at him as he walked toward her.

"I'm going to let one of your hands free so you can eat your food," he told her, setting the food and soda down on the floor before walking behind her chair to uncuff her. "You try anything and you'll sit in here with

no food, and I won't take you to use the bathroom

anymore. You'll have to piss on yourself right here in

the chair. Do we understand each other?"

"Why are you doing this?" Mia asked the detective.

"How much is Luther paying you to hold me here?"

Detective Harris uncuffed one of Mia's hands from

the chair in which she was seated as he handed her the

food.

"I'll be back in ten minutes to take you to the

bathroom," he said.

She watched as the detective left the room and shut

the door behind him. She wasted no time after hearing

the click of the door being locked, when she set the

food back down on the ground and dug out her phone

and turned it on.

She saw that Sean had tried calling her four times

as soon as the phone was powered up. Mia instantly

called him back, and heard his voice in the middle of

the first ring.

"Mia!"

Mia broke down as soon as she heard Sean's voice.

She could barely get out that she was kidnapped by two

Miami PD detectives who worked for Luther. She also

explained that she did not know where she was being

held.

"Mia, just stay calm," Sean told her. "I'm on my

way to you right now."

"What? How?"

"Just stay calm, Mia! I'm coming to get you out now!"

~ ~ ~

Sean found the location from Mia's signal. The signal led him to a two-story house, and he noticed there were four cars parked outside. Sean parked his 650i and climbed out as he carelessly slammed the car door. He truthfully wanted whoever was inside the house to know that he was outside.

He entered the front gate and walked up to the porch. He never saw anyone look out the window, but he was unsure if anyone looked out the peephole. Sean lightly knocked on the door and heard a football game playing on the television inside.

"Who is it?" a voice called out.

Sean only allowed those few words to escape the person on the other side of the peephole as he pulled out his .40 caliber from his back waist holster and swung it up and fired.

Boom!

~ ~ ~

Mia jumped at the sudden and all-too-familiar sound of gunfire. She instantly heard the repeated firing coming from somewhere inside the house as well as the sounds of men screaming in pain. She shot to her feet. She forgot about the chair she was cuffed to and began to drag it behind her as she rushed to the door to suddenly hear that all the shooting had stopped.

"What's going on?" Mia whispered to herself, standing beside the door and starting to feel really worried.

She caught the sound of something clicking and then what sounded like metal sliding and then another click, which she recognized as a gun being cocked and loaded.

She looked around for something to protect herself with, remembering the chair. Mia was just reaching for the chair when she heard someone trying to open the room door.

"Mia!"

Mia instantly recognized the voice as she screamed out to Sean to let him know she was inside the room.

Suddenly, she saw the door come flying inward from the kick Sean placed into it.

"Oh my God!" Mia cried, falling into him as Sean rushed over and hugged her. "Sean, I'm so happy to see you!"

"You okay?" he asked, pulling back to see that Mia's face was swollen and her eyes were black and blue.

"Baby, I'm fine!" Mia told him. "Just, please, get me out of this place, Sean!"

Sean freed Mia by shooting off the part of the cuffs that was still attached to the chair. He grabbed her hand and led her from the empty bedroom. She tried to keep up with Sean as he led her through what she now realized was a two-story house. Mia spotted the first body lying in front of the stairwell as the two of them came down.

Mia then saw more bodies as Sean led her to the front door, where Mia spotted both Detectives Robinson and Harris shot point blank in the head, each with a single bullet hole.

NINE

Mia contacted Jennifer as soon as Sean has gotten her into his BMW and was speeding out of the neighborhood. Mia broke down to her partner everything that had happened up until the point when Sean showed up and rescued her. She hung up with Jennifer after agreeing that they would meet up at her house.

"How did you find me?" Mia asked, after hanging up and focusing her attention completely onto Sean, all while slowly taking in his facial features.

"Your phone!" Sean answered, glancing over at her and seeing the questioning look on her face. "There's a GPS tracking chip in both your and Jennifer's phones."

"What?" Mia cried out loud. "Sean, what the hell are you talking about?"

He shifted his gaze again and looked from the road over to meet Mia's stare. He smirked as he began explaining how he had stolen both their phones a few months back and had tracking chips placed inside, so he would always be able to find them no matter where they were in the city.

"So let me guess!" Mia stated, shifting as much as she could in her seat to face Sean. "All this time that everything has been going on, you've been avoiding me, haven't you?"

"Actually, I haven't!" Sean admitted. "I've just been trying to focus, Mia!"

"Focus on what, Sean? You just up and disappeared without telling me nothing, and then I've been wondering what's been going on with this case against Simmons. Then I'm suddenly kidnapped and you literally reappear out of nowhere. Sean, you can't do this to me! How are we going to be in a relationship if I can't depend on you when I need you?"

"Mia, I've always been there when you need me!" he stated, taking his eyes off the road to look over at her. "I've just been getting my own head right and figuring out a few things."

"A few things like what, Sean?"

"I'll show you when it's time. I promise, Mia!"

~ ~ ~

"Hello!"

"Simmons, it's Paul. We've got a problem!"

"It's that FBI cunt! She somehow got away from the holding house. And get this: everyone I had at that house is dead. That bitch killed every last one of my men!"

"You're wrong, Paul. It wasn't the FBI woman. Mia's good at her job, but we both know this wasn't her work!"

"Then who the hell killed—!"

"Sean Carter!"

"You mean the bodyguard kid you told me about?

I thought he was long gone!"

"Apparently he isn't. But let me call you back, Paul.

I'm going to handle this."

"How?"

"I'm going to send a message to our friend Sean

that will help him decide whether or not he really wants

to fight this fight with his FBI cunt as you call her!"

~ ~ ~

"Mia!" Jennifer cried out as she came rushing

through the front door of Mia's apartment once the

door was answered by Sean. She found her best friend

and partner inside the kitchen holding a zip-lock bag

filled with ice cubes up against her face.

Jennifer saw Mia's face and instantly got upset. She

then started to question Mia, when she heard a painful yell and then her named being called.

Mia and Jennifer rushed from the kitchen and spotted Sean pressing their boss Agent Davis's face up against the wall, with his arm folded so far behind his back that it looked like it would break.

"Sean!" Mia and Jennifer screamed as they rushed over to break up the tussle between the two.

"Baby, let him go!" Mia begged as she pulled against Sean's arms. "Sean, that's my boss. Let him go!"

Mia got Sean to release Aaron as Mia and Jennifer saw to their boss. Mia walked over to Sean, who stood staring at her boss.

"Baby, relax! He's really our boss!"

"Somebody wanna explain to me what's going on and who the hell this son-of-a-bitch is? I'm seconds away from having him arrested for assaulting a Federal officer!" Agent Davis yelled while ranting and raving as he stared back angrily at the bastard that had just attacked him.

"Aaron, relax!" Jennifer spoke up this time. "Sean is Mia's fiancé and the one that got her back after she was kidnapped."

"Who the hell is he?" Aaron asked, looking back hatefully at Sean.

"His name is Sean Carter, and he's the reason we were able to—!"

"Wait!" Agent Davis stopped the conversation as

he looked from Mia to Sean. "You said his name is Sean what?"

"Carter!" Jennifer repeated, staring at her boss.

When Mia saw the look on his face, she asked, "Aaron, what's wrong?"

Still staring at the young man in front of him, Agent Davis spoke up again and asked, "Are you related to Jeffery Carter by any chance, boy?"

"He's my father!" Sean truthfully answered.

"I'll be damned!" Davis stated in disbelief while still staring at Sean. "I knew you looked familiar, boy. You look just like your father did at your age."

"Aaron, you know Sean's father?" Jennifer asked him while looking from Aaron over to Sean.

Agent Davis proceeded to explain to the three of them how he knew who Sean's father was. He then broke down that he was a part of the team that investigated Jeffery Carter a.k.a. "Big Jeff." Davis also truthfully admitted that his life as well as the lives of his boss at the time and seven other agents were saved because of Jeffery Carter.

"So you're part of the reason my father is spending seventy years in a federal prison/" Sean asked as he started toward Aaron, only for Mia to grab his arm.

"Sean!" she said in a pleading tone.

"I was part of the reason your father wasn't put to death, boy!" Agent Davis spoke up with no fear. "My boss wanted your father put to death, but I fought for

the seventy since it was all they were willing to offer

him."

"So I guess you think I owe you a thank you, huh?"

Sean asked, still mean-mugging the special agent.

"Boy, you don't owe me shit!" Davis replied. "I

was just doing my damn job!"

"Okay!" Jennifer spoke up, wanting to change the

subject and kill the tension in the air. "Let's focus on

this problem we're dealing with now. So how are we

going to stop Simmons and put him behind bars for

the rest of his life?"

"I'd rather put his ass to sleep!" Sean stated in all

seriousness.

"This is what we're going to do!" Agent Davis said

as he noticed the young Carter walking away at the ringing of the cell phone that he pulled from his pocket. "We're going to go after everyone we've got in connection with Simmons. We need to apply some real heavy—!"

"Sean!" Mia cried out, seeing Sean rush toward the front door. She took off behind him and caught up with Sean right outside. "Baby, what's wrong? Where are you going?"

"Mia, something's happened to my father! I gotta go!" Sean explained before jogging off.

Deciding right then and there, Mia called out to Jennifer and yelled that she was going with Sean as she took off behind her man. She wanted to be where he was when he needed her.

~ ~ ~

Sean and Mia reached Tracy's house twenty minutes later to find everyone already there. The two of them were let inside by his Aunt Toni, who was in tears, only to throw her arms around his neck once she realized who he was.

Sean then walked his crying auntie into the house as Mia closed and locked the door behind them. Sean found the rest of the family inside the den together when he walked into the room.

"Sean!" Tracy cried at the sight of her stepson.

She then saw her daughter take off from her seat and run straight into her brother. Sean hugged and picked up his sister and carried her over to where Tracy and Ma'Pearl sat together. He bent down and kissed and hugged Tracy with his free left hand and then did the same with his grandmother.

"So what happened?" Sean asked as he sat on the floor beside Tracy, with his sister curled up beside him. "How's Big Jeff doing?"

"They say ya dad was set up, man!" Marvin spoke up from beside Toni at the left of Sean. "We was told some type of huge fight broke out after ya dad was stabbed, but word is that ya dad killed two dudes and sent three to an outside hospital before he was helped out of the chow hall by two inmates who I was told were soldiers of his."

"How you know all of this?" Mia asked, drawing attention to herself.

"Who the hell are you?" Marvin asked, balling up his face as he stared at Mia.

"Relax, Marvin!" Sean spoke up. "She's with me, but that is a good question though. How *do* you know all this?"

Marvin shot the female with Sean another look before he said, "I've got a few friends out there where your dad's at, and they told me how the shit went down."

"Who'd your friend say was responsible for this shit happening?" Sean asked Marvin just as the doorbell sounded off throughout the house.

"Nobody really knows who's behind the bullshit, Sean!" Marvin told him as Toni got up to answer the door. "But my people think it was a hit set up for Big Jeff!"

"Why?" Tracy asked.

"That's what everybody is trying to figure out now!" Marvin stated just as Toni and another figure walked into the den.

"Michael," Tracy cried out, standing from the sofa beside her mother-in-law and approaching her husband's friend to hug him. "Thank you for coming!" she told him as she walked him over to the couch and then returned to her seat beside Ma'Pearl.

"Michael, tell us what you found out!" Tony spoke

up to her family friend.

"Well, I do know that Jeffery is going to be okay," Michael started. "I found out that he was stabbed once in the side and twice in the back, and he's at the hospital now."

"Who did it?" Sean asked again.

"Ummm, Sean!" Michael started as he stood back up to his feet.

~ ~ ~

"Talk, Detective!" Sean told Michael once the two of them were outside and standing at Michael's car.

"First, I spoke with your father, Sean. He wants to see you, and he told me to tell you that whoever you're pissing off out there, they're sending you a warning through him. He's not concerned about himself, but more so your sister and Tracy. He told me to tell you to either deal with your problem or stop fucking with whoever it is you're messing with!"

"Luther Simmons?" Sean asked as he held Michael's eyes and saw the retired detective nod his head in agreement.

"That's who set up the hit on your father, Sean!" Michael admitted. "I know this because I was getting a meeting set up with Captain Sinclair to meet with your cousin when I heard the captain agree to see if he could get a few of his guys to find some people at the prison to take out your father."

"He said all this in front of you, huh?" Sean asked

him.

"He doesn't know my relationship with this family, Sean!" Michael explained. "I really didn't know that Captain Sinclair was even involved with Simmons, but I do know that Simmons isn't in town anymore."

"What do you mean? Where the fuck is he?"

"I mean that Simmons has gone into hiding. But word is that he's put $1 million on your head, Sean! There have been photos of you passed around, and soon you're going to have every hustler, jack boy, and hired killa in the city after you, Sean!"

Not really worried about that, Sean changed the subject and asked, "Can you do me a favor?"

"What's up, son?" Michael asked him.

Sean explained to the retired detective what he needed him to do, and very soon. He then dug out his keys once he was finished. He pulled off two different keys and handed them to Michael and said, "If anything happens to any one of them, I promise I'll find you. We clear, Detective?"

"Perfectly!" Michael answered with a smile as he stared at his old friend's twin son.

TEN

Sean took a trip out to the hospital where his father was being held, after taking care of everything back home with his family. Sean was allowed into his father's hospital room, where he saw two armed guards posted inside with him.

"Can we have some privacy?" Sean asked, looking behind him at the officer in charge.

Sean saw the officer in charge motion for the two guards to leave the room. Sean then turned his attention back to this father and saw the old man smiling at him from his hospital bed.

"What's up, Dad?" Sean said, walking over to the

bed and bending down to hug him. "How you feeling?"

"Too old for this shit!" Big Jeff answered as he sat up inside the bed before saying, "I hear you're out there causing trouble and got some people really pissed off with you, Son."

"I hear a lot of stuff, Dad!" Sean replied with a smile.

Big Jeff shook his head and was still smiling.

"Sean, look! I'm not exactly sure what you're into out there, because Mike won't tell me because he's truly afraid of what you'd do to him. But he has told me you got this clown Luther Simmons spooked out of his mind, and that's why he went into hiding. How? I have no idea, but I will tell you this, Sean, Luther isn't someone you want to half-step with. Because he's got people all over willing to help him because of the shit he does. So when you catch him, do not hesitate to put a bullet in his ass. If I had known what I know now, I would have killed his ass when I had the chance."

"Wait!" Sean stated. "You mean you know Luther Simmons?"

"Mike ain't tell you, huh?"

"Tell me what?"

Big Jeff laughed lightly as he said, "Me and Luther started out together, Sean! He used to be a friend and business partner, but he got jealous and greedy; and in the end he had me set up, and the Feds ran down on me and left me with seventy years. I'm still fighting to get off my ass!"

"So Luther set you up, huh?" Sean repeated, seeing his father nod his head. "That's much more of a reason to find his ass!"

"What are you gonna do when you find him, Sean? Kill him?"

"Naw!" Sean said with a smirk. "I'ma murder his ass, Dad!"

~ ~ ~

Sean left his father's hospital room after spending another hour with him. He then made it back to his car where he called Mia.

"Hello!"

"Mia, it's Sean. Where you at?"

"Still at the office. We just got out of our meeting, and to answer your question before you ask it, no, the FBI isn't putting out a warrant for Simmons, because there's really no probable cause for his arrest!"

"I figured that much!"

"So what now?"

"I want you to consider what you and I spoke about the other night!"

"Sean, I've already told you that I'm not running and hiding from Simmons or nobody else! I'm staying right here to do my job!"

Sean sighed deeply and then said, "All right, just do me a favor, Mia!"

"What's that?"

"Wear that vest I gave you. I don't trust the bullshit the FBI issued you. Do that for me!   "

"Okay, Sean," Mia agreed with the deep sigh of her own. "I'll wear the vest, baby."

~ ~ ~

After making it back to Miami by 7:20 that evening, Sean put a call in to Michael Brown and let him know that he was back. He then made his way across town to the Miami Subs where he and Mia sometimes grabbed a sandwich. He pulled into the parking lot to see how long the drive-through line was.

Once he was inside the restaurant and saw the six-man line, Sean fell in at the back of the line and stared up at the overhead menu, when his cell phone rang.

He saw that his cousin Tony was on the other end.

"What's up, Cousin?"

"Yo, where you at, Sean?"

"At the Miami Subs at 441 and 194th Street. What's

up, though?"

Sean listened to his cousin, but peeped the guys

that were four spaces in front of him in line but staring

back at him. Sean continued with his phone call with

Tony, only hanging up after his cousin told him that he

was coming to meet him.

Sean then noticed the two guys still watching him,

even after they walked off after getting their food.

Sean placed his order and then paid, and then

stepped to the side and waited a few minutes until his

food was brought out to him. He walked over to a table

next to the window that overlooked the parking lot. He

also peeped the two guys that were inside the Chevy

Impala that was parked just a few spaces down from

where he was parked.

He saw T.J.'s Crown Vic turn into the parking lot

a little while later. Sean sat eating and watching as Tony

and T.J. climbed from their car once they parked.

"Tony!" Sean called out as soon as his cousin and

T.J. walked inside.

"What's up, Cuz?" Tony said as he and T.J. walked

up to Sean's table.

Sean shook up with both guys, picked his sub back

up, and then asked, "So why y'all still out here? Everybody else is already gone."

"Cuz, no disrespect, but I ain't on that hiding shit!" Tony told Sean. "This is my city, and whatever happens is gonna happen!"

Sean nodded his head after listening to his cousin and then shifted his eyes to the window looking back at the Impala and seeing the two guys still waiting.

~ ~ ~

After leaving the restaurant after finishing his food, Sean walked out to his car as both Tony and T.J. headed to the Crown Vic.

Sean hit the locks and climbed into his i8. He glanced over at the Impala and saw the passengers still watching him as he was bending down to climb into the car.

Sean swiftly closed the door instead of getting inside. He took off from the driver's door as he came up behind the Impala that was now running. He pulled out his Ruger and then spun off onto the driver's side. He walked up onto the driver's door and saw both the driver and passenger staring out the passenger window at his car. He also saw that both of them were holding burners and waiting.

Sean smiled as he said, "Looking for somebody, fellas?"

"Oh shit!" was all Sean allowed the driver to say as both would-be hit men spun around in their seats to see him standing there pointing his Ruger straight at them.

Boom! Boom! Boom! Boom! Boom!

Sean dumped off into the Impala and killed both would-be killers. He then took off from their car and returned to his car and jumped inside before the first person exited Miami Subs to see what was going on.

ELEVEN

Sean made it back to his building with no more problems. He entered his condo and heard his television playing, when he knew for sure that he had turned it off before he left. He gently and quietly closed the front door with his left arm while pulling his .40 caliber with his right from his back holster.

He slowly walked through the front of his condo and saw no one before he made his way toward the back where he heard music playing on low. He followed the sound to his bedroom and saw the door opened. He smiled at the sight of Mia in only her panties and no bra. She was standing at his bed about to put on one of his T-shirts.

"You look good naked!" he said, which caused Mia to move faster than he thought she could as she snatched up her Glock that was lying next to her clothes on the bed.

"Sean!" Mia said with a sigh of relief after seeing it was him. "Boy, I almost shot you!"

"You probably would have gotten me, too!" Sean told her with a smile as he entered the room and walked over to her. "Any time I see you naked, and I lose the ability to think clearly."

"Is that so?" Mia stated, smiling as she wrapped her arms loosely around Sean's neck. He gently picked her up and softly laid her down onto the bed, only to position himself between her legs as they began kissing.

Sean then got Mia out of what little she had on and then got out of his own clothes. He then set his .40 caliber, Glock, and Ruger on the bedside table, before climbing back into the bed and moving between her legs.

Sean felt Mia reach between them and take his manhood in her hand. He held her eyes as she led him to her opening.

"Condoms, Mia!"

"I've been taking the pill!" she told him as she wrapped her legs around him, causing Sean to slide slowly inside of her.

~ ~ ~

Sean was soundless beside Mia when he heard his front door being kicked in. He rolled out of bed, grabbed both his Ruger and Glock, and got up onto his knees.

Boom! Boom! Boom!

Sean heard the shots fired and looked to his left to see Mia in shooter's stance with her Glock smoking.

Sean had a small smile on his face as he said, "Get dressed!"

Sean dropped two more intruders that appeared in front of his bedroom door, just as Mia slid across the bed and tossed him his clothes. She took position while he got dressed. Sean then snatched up his .40 caliber and slid it into the back of his pants, just as more shots were fired.

Sean looked back to see another unwanted guest now sliding slowly down the wall next to the doorway.

Sean gave Mia a kiss and then nodded toward the door.

"Let's get the fuck outta here!"

They left the bedroom and made their way toward the front of the condo. They saw things broken, but no one else was inside the place. Mia grabbed Sean's arm to stop him and said, "Baby, my phone! Let me get it out of the den real fast!"

Mia rushed off to retrieve her phone from the den as she explained to Sean. She then turned away from the coffee table where her phone was sitting. Just as she started back toward the front door, she saw a figure appear behind Sean.

"Sean, behind you!" she screamed as she sprinted toward him.

Sean spun around at Mia's warning, just as a shot was fired. He felt the pain explode from his side but ignored it as he grabbed and slammed the intruder back against the wall and inside the hallway. He smashed his elbow on his left arm into the intruder's neck with such force that he heard the breaking of the man's neck.

"Sean!" Mia cried again as she reached his side just in time to see the intruder's body drop dead to the ground at Sean's feet. She looked up at his face to see him still staring down at the dead intruder. "Baby, you okay?"

"Shiiiiitt!" Sean quickly got out as he grabbed Mia's hand when she grabbed his side.

"What's wrong?" Mia asked. When she looked down, she noticed that Sean was bleeding. "Oh my God, Sean! You've been shot!"

"I'll be fine," he told her as he gently pushed her in the direction of the elevator. "We got to get out of here."

"Are you okay?" Mia asked again while walking up the hallway. Her concern was shown on her face and in her tone as she spoke to him.

"I'm fine, Mia!" Sean once again told her as the two of them stopped at the elevator. He began to hit the button when he noticed that not one but both elevators were rising instead of lowering. "Come on! We gotta

take the stairwell!"

"What?" Mia asked.

She quickly went silent after seeing the familiar

expression on Sean's face. She followed alongside him

at a quick pace, once he began jogging down the

hallway to the stairwell door.

"Get behind me!" he told her once the two of them

entered the stairwell. "Watch my back."

Sean ignored the pain that he felt in his side where

he was hit. He then made his way cautiously yet swiftly

down the stairs while sensing Mia close behind him as

he made his way down to the parking garage.

Sean pushed open the door just enough to be

allowed to look out into the garage. He then pushed the door open farther once he was sure no one was inside.

"Let's go!" he told Mia as the two of them began walking from the stairwell into the parking garage.

They made their way deeper into the garage and spotted the 650i. Sean called over for Mia to drive. He tossed her the keys as he made his way around to the passenger side. Once Mia got the doors unlocked inside the car, Sean went straight to taking off his shirt and ignoring the pain that shot through his side as he pulled the shirt up over his head.

"Baby, are you okay?" Mia asked for the third time.

Even though she could see the hurt in Sean's eyes,

his face displayed that he was calm and okay.

"Mia, I'm okay. Shit!" Sean growled as he was looking over the wound, touching only around the side but still feeling the pain. "It's good. The bullet just ripped straight through."

Mia tried to watch the road and pay attention to Sean as she drove away from the apartment building. She never noticed the two dark-colored Crown Vics that were parked across the street in front of the parking garage entrance/exit or when both cars fueled off behind the BMW. She began to ask Sean another question when the shooting suddenly started.

"What the hell!" Mia screamed, ducking down after the shots began jumping when a few bullets slammed repeatedly into the back window, although it did not break.

"Just relax and drive!" Sean told her, looking through the side mirror to see the two Crown Vics trailing them with shooters hanging out of the windows. He forgot about his wound and turned his focus to both his .40 and his Glock and checked both magazines. "Where's your gun?" he asked after seeing he was almost empty in one and completely out in the other.

"It's in my lap!" Mia answered, but then added, "But I'm outta bullets, Sean!"

Sean sighed but was not worried as he leaned over and reached across Mia to press the cruise control button, only to hear a humming sound. He then looked over at the stereo system just as the facepiece slowly raised to allow the chrome .45 automatic to appear.

"What the hell!" Mia yelled after seeing the hidden compartment Sean had just opened.

She sat and watched him pull out the automatic and then look over to her and say, "You think you can get some distance from them?"

"In this thing. Hell yeah!" Mia assured him with a smile.

"Gimme a three-minute head start, and then pull over!" Sean told her, sighing deeply as he focused on forgetting the pain in his side.

Mia stared at Sean, even though he was not paying

her any attention at the moment.

She could not believe what the hell she just heard Sean ask her to do, when she yelled out, "Sean, are you outta your damn mind? I am not pulling over so you can—!"

"Mia!" Sean yelled with his voice booming as he cut off his hard-headed girlfriend. "Just do what I ask!"

"Sean, we need to just call for backup," she continued, trying to convince him.

"Mia, I already warned you!" he told her as he sat staring at her. "We tried things your way the first time and it didn't work, so now it's my turn. Are you going to do as I asked you to do?"

Mia stared at him for a few moments and shook

her head, but she did not say anything else as she focused on the road.

Doing as Sean asked, she pushed the 650i up to 70 mph and easily pulled away from the two trailing Crown Vics. She then hit a few turns; and when both Crown Vics were out of sight, she did as she was told and pulled the car over.

"What are you going to do now, Sean?" Mia asked after putting the BMW into park and then turning to face him.

Sean looked over to meet Mia's eyes and saw the concern but surprisingly no worry, which allowed him to believe that she fully trusted him to take care of things. He reached across over to Mia and gently ran the back of his hand down alongside her face before

saying, "Do you trust me, Mia?"

"Sean, what are you—?"

"Do you trust me?" he asked again, after cutting

her off.

Mia sighed deeply and replied, "Yes, Sean, I trust

you fully!"

Sean nodded his head and showed a small smile.

He had just winked his eye at her when the screaming

of car tires drew his attention around and he faced

frontward. He watched as the two Crown Vics sped

down the street as he and Mia sat inside the BMW

parked in the middle of the road. Sean said nothing

more, but opened the car door and calmly climbed out.

Standing in the middle of the road watching as both cars spend directly toward them, Sean calmly held up the .45 automatic. With a calm and relaxed mind, he aimed the gun and fired rapid but extremely accurate shots, shooting through the front windshields, first taking out the driver of the Crown Vic on his right and then the one on his left.

"Oh my God!" Mia cried out in a whisper when she saw Sean's shooting skills that caused both cars to lose control and slam into each other.

Sean climbed out of the car after the two Crown Vics collided. Mia began to ask him a question, only to see him begin walking off and heading toward the two cars.

"Sean, what are you doing?" she called out, only to be ignored as he continued walking over to the cars.

Boom! Boom! Boom! Boom!

Mia jumped slightly after a shot was fired first into one Crown Vic. Mia stood watching in total shock when she saw Sean walk from one car to the other, killing whoever was left breathing inside of them.

Mia was unsure exactly what to think of the situation, but not about her feelings toward Sean as she watched him walk back to his BMW. Mia waited until he was back over in front of the passenger side door and looked at her.

She then said, "So this is your way of dealing with our problem, Sean?"

"I'll answer that when all of this is over and Luther is in front of us dead or alive!" Sean explained to Mia while looking back over at the two Crown Vics and staring a few moments as thoughts flowed through his mind concerning Mia's question.

To be continued . . . .

To order books, please fill out the order form below:
To order films please go to www.good2gofilms.com

Name: _____

Address:_____

City: _____ State: _____ Zip Code: _____

Phone:_____

Email:_____

Method of Payment: Check   VISA   MASTERCARD

Credit Card#:_____

Name as it appears on card: _____

Signature: _____

Item Name	Price	Qty	Amount
48 Hours to Die – Silk White	$14.99		
A Hustler's Dream - Ernest Morris	$14.99		
A Hustler's Dream 2 - Ernest Morris	$14.99		
A Thug's Devotion – J. L. Rose and J. M. McMillon	$14.99		
All Eyes on Tommy Gunz – Warren Holloway	$14.99		
Black Reign – Ernest Morris	$14.99		
Bloody Mayhem Down South – Trayvon Jackson	$14.99		
Bloody Mayhem Down South 2 – Trayvon Jackson	$14.99		
Business Is Business – Silk White	$14.99		
Business Is Business 2 – Silk White	$14.99		
Business Is Business 3 – Silk White	$14.99		
Cash In Cash Out – Assa Raymond Baker	$14.99		
Cash In Cash Out 2 - Assa Raymond Baker	$14.99		
Childhood Sweethearts – Jacob Spears	$14.99		
Childhood Sweethearts 2 – Jacob Spears	$14.99		
Childhood Sweethearts 3 - Jacob Spears	$14.99		
Childhood Sweethearts 4 - Jacob Spears	$14.99		
Connected To The Plug – Dwan Marquis Williams	$14.99		
Connected To The Plug 2 – Dwan Marquis Williams	$14.99		
Connected To The Plug 3 – Dwan Williams	$14.99		
Deadly Reunion – Ernest Morris	$14.99		
Dream's Life – Assa Raymond Baker	$14.99		

Flipping Numbers – Ernest Morris	$14.99		
Flipping Numbers 2 – Ernest Morris	$14.99		
He Loves Me, He Loves You Not - Mychea	$14.99		
He Loves Me, He Loves You Not 2 - Mychea	$14.99		
He Loves Me, He Loves You Not 3 - Mychea	$14.99		
He Loves Me, He Loves You Not 4 – Mychea	$14.99		
He Loves Me, He Loves You Not 5 – Mychea	$14.99		
Kings of the Block – Dwan Willams	$14.99		
Kings of the Block 2 – Dwan Willams	$14.99		
Lord of My Land – Jay Morrison	$14.99		
Lost and Turned Out – Ernest Morris	$14.99		
Love Hates Violence – De'Wayne Maris	$14.99		
Love Hates Violence 2 – De'Wayne Maris	$14.99		
Love Hates Violence 3 – De'Wayne Maris	$14.99		
Love Hates Violence 4 – De'Wayne Maris	$14.99		
Married To Da Streets – Silk White	$14.99		
M.E.R.C. - Make Every Rep Count Health and Fitness	$14.99		
Mercenary In Love – J.L. Rose & J.L. Turner	$14.99		
Mercenary In Love 2 – J.L. Rose & J.L. Turner	$14.99		
Money Make Me Cum – Ernest Morris	$14.99		
My Besties – Asia Hill	$14.99		
My Besties 2 – Asia Hill	$14.99		
My Besties 3 – Asia Hill	$14.99		
My Besties 4 – Asia Hill	$14.99		
My Boyfriend's Wife - Mychea	$14.99		
My Boyfriend's Wife 2 – Mychea	$14.99		
My Brothers Envy – J. L. Rose	$14.99		
My Brothers Envy 2 – J. L. Rose	$14.99		
Naughty Housewives – Ernest Morris	$14.99		
Naughty Housewives 2 – Ernest Morris	$14.99		
Naughty Housewives 3 – Ernest Morris	$14.99		

Naughty Housewives 4 – Ernest Morris	$14.99		
Never Be The Same – Silk White	$14.99		
Shades of Revenge – Assa Raymond Baker	$14.99		
Slumped – Jason Brent	$14.99		
Someone's Gonna Get It – Mychea	$14.99		
Stranded – Silk White	$14.99		
Supreme & Justice – Ernest Morris	$14.99		
Supreme & Justice 2 – Ernest Morris	$14.99		
Supreme & Justice 3 – Ernest Morris	$14.99		
Tears of a Hustler - Silk White	$14.99		
Tears of a Hustler 2 - Silk White	$14.99		
Tears of a Hustler 3 - Silk White	$14.99		
Tears of a Hustler 4- Silk White	$14.99		
Tears of a Hustler 5 – Silk White	$14.99		
Tears of a Hustler 6 – Silk White	$14.99		
The Last Love Letter – Warren Holloway	$14.99		
The Last Love Letter 2 – Warren Holloway	$14.99		
The Panty Ripper - Reality Way	$14.99		
The Panty Ripper 3 – Reality Way	$14.99		
The Solution – Jay Morrison	$14.99		
The Teflon Queen – Silk White	$14.99		
The Teflon Queen 2 – Silk White	$14.99		
The Teflon Queen 3 – Silk White	$14.99		
The Teflon Queen 4 – Silk White	$14.99		
The Teflon Queen 5 – Silk White	$14.99		
The Teflon Queen 6 - Silk White	$14.99		
The Vacation – Silk White	$14.99		
Tied To A Boss - J.L. Rose	$14.99		
Tied To A Boss 2 - J.L. Rose	$14.99		
Tied To A Boss 3 - J.L. Rose	$14.99		
Tied To A Boss 4 - J.L. Rose	$14.99		

Tied To A Boss 5 - J.L. Rose	$14.99		
Time Is Money - Silk White	$14.99		
Tomorrow's Not Promised – Robert Torres	$14.99		
Tomorrow's Not Promised 2 – Robert Torres	$14.99		
Two Mask One Heart – Jacob Spears and Trayvon Jackson	$14.99		
Two Mask One Heart 2 – Jacob Spears and Trayvon Jackson	$14.99		
Two Mask One Heart 3 – Jacob Spears and Trayvon Jackson	$14.99		
Wrong Place Wrong Time – Silk White	$14.99		
Young Goonz – Reality Way	$14.99		
Subtotal:			
Tax:			
Shipping (Free) U.S. Media Mail:			
Total:			

Make Checks Payable To:
Good2Go Publishing
7311 W Glass Lane,
Laveen, AZ 85339